Big Night

Big Night

A Novel with Recipes by
JOSEPH TROPIANO

Based on the Screenplay by
STANLEY TUCCI &
JOSEPH TROPIANO

 ST. MARTIN'S GRIFFIN ◑◐ NEW YORK

Library of Congress Cataloging-in-Publication Data

Tropiano, Joseph.
    Big night / by Joseph Tropiano.
        p.   cm.
    ISBN 0-312-14844-5
    I. Title.
    PS3570.R588B54   1996
    813'.54—dc20   96-19762
                                                              CIP

First St. Martin's Griffin Edition: October 1996

10   9   8   7   6   5   4   3   2   1

For my grandparents,

VINCENZO AND CONCETTA TROPIANO
and
GIOVANNI AND MARIA COLANGELO

INTRODUCTION

The film *Big Night* was born first of a desire on the part of my cousin Stanley Tucci and myself to create a movie in which Italians are portrayed not as clichéd, spaghetti-serving sentimentalists, nor as murderous, back-stabbing Mafiosi, but as the complex, difficult, funny, stubborn, wonderful people they are. As an actor, Stanley has often been typecast as the Mafia soldier or menacing mug, due to his extraordinary ability to tap the dark side of humanity. In my life, I have encountered well-meaning and otherwise intelligent people who have laughingly suggested, when I was faced with a difficult landlord or an obnoxious coworker, that I could simply contact a relative who could "fix up everything." Both of us had had just about enough of such stereotyping when we sat down to start the screenplay in 1991. It took us four years, off and on, to complete.

Certainly there have been American films that have portrayed Italians and Italian-Americans humanely, decently, and realistically (*Moonstruck* comes to mind). But even today, in our "politically correct" time, it is rare that an Italian character shows up on-screen without the assumption that he or she is linked to violence and criminality. One recent film, Gus Van Sant and Buck Henry's black comedy *To Die For*, featured an Italian-American restaurant-owning family whose son (played by Matt Dillon) was murdered through the machinations of his insanely ambitious wife (played by Nicole Kidman). To avenge his son's murder, the otherwise upstanding restaurant owner simply called in a killer to knock off Nicole, as if the Mafia, or underworld, were some kind of Italian-American National Guard.

Like any other lover of the movies, I would be the first to proclaim Francis Coppola's *Godfather* trilogy and Martin Scorsese's *Mean Streets* and *Goodfellas* as film masterpieces that transformed a small slice of Italian life into brilliant meditations on family ties, power, and success. But clearly, these films (and countless others in their wake) have also left a black mark on the public's idea of who and what Italians are. To some extent, Italian-American characters on-screen are now already guilty of an affiliation with the Mafia before the movie even begins, and as such they carry the burden of proving otherwise.

Stan and I were sure that there was room on film's broad canvas to highlight some of the myriad other facets of the Italian character. These include a love of and talent for the arts; the difficulty, shared by all immigrant groups, of balancing the desire to fit into the larger American mosaic with the need to cling to Old World ties; and the sheer hard work that, for decades, Italian-Americans have engaged in — without resorting to violence — to stake their claim for the American Dream. I can state with all authority that no member of our respective extended families is now or has ever been affiliated with the Mob.

As kids, Stan and I would see each other frequently on Sundays when our large family got together for afternoon dinners at our grandparents' home. There was usually an occasion to celebrate — the birth of yet another cousin or a birthday or an anniversary — but we didn't really need a reason. The point was, first, to be together, and, second, to eat, which in our family was usually one and the same. At the dinner table laden with dishes prepared by our mothers, aunts, and grandmother, the conversation would inevitably turn to meals we had eaten in the past, about what we were eating at the moment, and what we would like to eat in the future.

Not all the talk revolved around food, of course. After dinner, stuffed to the eyeballs, Stanley and I would inevitably take a walk around my suburban Westchester neighborhood and talk about movies. So it's not surprising we grew up to write a film about food. In our late twenties, we each spent a good amount of time watching European films—especially Italian films—at revival houses, on video, wherever we could find them, and discussing what we saw. At the risk of overgeneralizing, the European style of filmmaking, which emphasizes characters over plot and permits them the time to tell their story, strongly influenced the writing of the script and the shooting and editing of *Big Night*.

Growing up next door to my paternal grandparents, I watched my *nonna* cook meals that I loved eating, but, honestly, had little appreciation for at the time. What I know now is that, like much of Italian cooking, many of my grandmother's dishes were completely specific to Cittanova, the small mountain village in the southern region of Calabria from which her family and my grandfather emigrated. (She makes the most incredible fried cookies, which I have never seen or read about elsewhere.) I learned at an early age, without realizing it, that cooking is as individual a means of expression as painting or sculpting or directing movies in which the Mafia plays a central role.

Which brings me to the second inspiration for *Big Night:* the difficult dance of art and money. The conflict between maintaining individual artistic expression and bowing to the demands of the marketplace is one that is as old as the ages and one that has long been on Stan's mind as an actor and mine as a writer. When Pascal counsels Secondo in the film, "Give to people what they want—then you can give them what you want," his remark is based on an honest assessment of what, for the most part, works in America. This is generally the case in the realm of entertainment, where safer is better, mass appeal is always more lucrative, homogenization beats out specificity every time, and what everybody wants is what everybody knows and what everybody knows is what everybody wants and—well, you get the idea.

I think *Big Night* does a better job of raising questions about the relationship between art and money than answering them—for the simple reason that there are no easy answers. But at a time when public support for the arts is either waning (witness the sad, slow death of the National Endowment for the Arts), or all tied up with politics, or under siege by the antiquated, irrelevant, so-called "moral" standards of the right, the questions need to be asked again and again. Is there a price on individual artistic expression? Does it have "value"? Can we afford *not* to support it? How many "Primos" are out there, struggling with their art, who will never get the chance to have their "big night"?

Because *Big Night* was an independently produced film, I was able to be involved in its creation as much as I wanted to be, which meant I could hang around on the set and get in everybody's way. We were blessed not only with a supportive funder in Rysher Entertainment, but with a devoted production team, cast and crew, and editing and postproduction staff, who worked the proverbial long hours for only-the-most-basic pay, most often with humor, and always with support for what we were trying to make—an entertaining film with something on its mind. The very lucky outcome was that Stan, codirector Campbell Scott, and I were able to put the vision we carried around in our heads for four years up on the screen, virtually without the kinds of compromises that Pascal insists are the necessary ingredients in the recipe for success.

A few words on the recipes in this book. I'm not a professional chef, and my experience in the kitchen has been limited to what I've cobbled from family, friends, and cookbooks, with a few dashes of my own invention thrown in. I've tried to include recipes for foods or dishes that make an appearance (either starring or cameo) in the film. For the most part, the recipes in this book are fairly simple and do not require a great deal of experience, with the possible exceptions of the directions for making fresh pasta by hand and for making *risotto*. (Both of these, like baking great bread, take a fair amount of practice to master—get yourself a good cookbook or find someone to teach you if you're serious.) I hope they reflect the easy freshness of Italian *trattoria*-style cooking and the simplicity we strove for in creating *Big Night*.

A lack of simplicity is one of the reasons you won't find a recipe here for *timpano*, the pasta-in-pastry dish that Primo and Secondo serve as the centerpiece of their dinner. This recipe, which comes from the Tucci family cookbook and is specific to their village of origin in Calabria, is not only long but somewhat complicated. It's also the subject of considerable, friendly disagreement and discussion within the family as to what amounts and types of ingredients go into it and as to the exact procedures required to make a truly "authentic" *timpano*. In short, a definitive version of the recipe is hard to pin down and I wouldn't presume to publish one. Perhaps someday the Tuccis will let the world in on their secret.

When speaking to audiences at film festivals and in talks with people who have seen *Big Night*, I'm often asked what I think happens to Primo and Secondo *after* the end of the story. Do they continue in America or do they return to Italy? Do they stay together or do they go their separate ways? Obviously, if Stanley and I thought we knew, we would have carried the story further. My best answer is that

Introduction

there *is* an ending and it's no more complex than this: Primo and Secondo have each other, for now. Those of us who are fortunate to have close family, a spouse, a lover, or good friends to whom we are happily and often maddeningly tied, know that, sometimes, that's all we can ask for—and, sometimes, it's enough.

J.T.
May 1996
New York City

THE RECIPES

In heaven, roast geese fly round with gravy boats in their bills; tarts grow wild like sunflowers; everywhere there are brooks of bouillon and champagne, everywhere trees on which napkins flutter, and you eat and wipe your lips and eat again without injury to your stomach; you sing psalms, or flirt with the dear, delicate little angels.

—*Heinrich Heine*

$\mathscr{Big}$
$\mathscr{Night}$

Chapter One

Primo's Tomato Sauce

Il Ragù di Primo

Finely chop one carrot, a rib of celery, a garlic clove, and a small onion. Put these in a heavy-bottomed saucepan or skillet and add 3 tablespoons of extra-virgin olive oil and salt to taste. Cook over medium heat until the vegetables are soft, about 3 or 4 minutes. (If you don't want to make a meat sauce, skip the next part.)

If you want to make this sauce with meat, add ½ pound of ground beef (you can also use pork, or veal, or any combination of the three) to the pan and mix with the vegetables. Cook over low heat until the meat is browned, about 5 minutes.

Open two 28-ounce cans of Italian tomatoes and add to the pan. (Brands canned in San Marzano, Italy, are often a good choice.) You can use either crushed tomatoes or whole tomatoes; if using whole, break up the tomatoes in the pan with a fork. Add a dried bay leaf and 2 tablespoons of chopped Italian flat-leaf parsley, if you like. Cover the pan and cook for about 20 minutes or until the sauce is thickened, stirring occasionally. Serve with your favorite pasta.

Secondo

"*Prova.*"

My brother holds out a spoonful of his *ragù* to me and I dip my finger in the sauce and then into my mouth to taste. "*C'è bisogno di più sale?*" he asks.

"What?" I say to him. I have to push Primo to talk in the language of our new country. This makes him go crazy, but here we are in America two years already and he must learn to speak English better.

Primo scowls at me and says, "More salt?"

"No," I say and smile at him. The sauce is fine. Primo's sauce always is fine.

I see him ignore me and he adds more salt to the sauce cooking on the stove. Then he points at the garlic I am chopping on the big block across the stove from him.

"No too fine."

I look at him. *Madonna miseria.*

"Well, sometimes you cut it too fine, Secondo," he says, "and then all you taste is the garlic." He always has to get something in. I think this is because he is my older brother and he thinks he has to teach me all the time. But I know I am the one who teaches him.

I do not pay any attention to him and I scrape the chopped-up garlic off the board into a bowl.

"Okay," I say. "Let's go, five minutes."

"*Io sono pronto,*" Primo says. Our busboy, Cristiano, comes through the swinging doors of the kitchen, carrying a stack of ashtrays he needs to wash. Cristiano is a good boy, he does a good job, but I think I have to push him to work hard anyway. In America, you can get ahead, but you must work very hard.

"Cristiano, let's go, chop chop, we open in five minutes," I tell him.

"Oh my God I can't believe, *mucho trabajo, poco dinero*," he says. Cristiano comes from Puerto Rico, and he speaks in English even worse than my brother. I never understand what he says when he talks in Spanish and I think he likes this.

Our kitchen is not like what you find in most restaurants in America. It is more like the kitchen in our uncle's *trattoria* in Italy, where me and my brother come from two years ago, in 1955. Our stove has six burners and two ovens and it is not up against the wall, but it sits right in the middle of the room. This makes much more sense I think because then the chef can move around more easy and he can see where everything is in the kitchen instead of looking at the wall.

At the back of the stove we have a long chopping block for chopping the tomatoes, garlic, onion, celery, whatever Primo needs to cook. Over the stove hangs a big metal rack with all the pots and pans. If you look at the pots and pans close you can see there are dents and scratches in them because when Primo gets mad he sometimes throws a pot at the wall or the ceiling. I tell him we are not made of money and pots cost us a lot. But when he gets mad I think the best thing is to be someplace else.

When we buy this place it is in pretty bad shape. I have to fix the roof over the kitchen because it have a hole. I scrub the tile on the kitchen floor and the white tiles that come up the walls halfway. Then I paint the walls and the ceiling and I scour all the tables with boiling water to make clean. I make it look pretty good. But some things I can't fix myself, like the water pipes. *Madonna miseria,* they are very old, so old I think they were put in when the Roman Empire build the first water pipes or whatever it was they build to carry the water.

When Cristiano turns on the faucet to wash the ashtrays, the pipes under the sink start to rattle like the volcano Etna is going to blow. They spit out air but no water comes out. This goddamn thief plumber! He just was come here two days ago and he said he fixed everything up! We all look at the sink and then finally, the water comes out in a stream.

"Remind me to call the plumber to come back tomorrow so I can kill him," I say to Primo. I wipe my fingers with a piece of lemon to get off the smell of the garlic. I don't mind the *aglio,* but I do not think my customers want to smell this on my hands when I am serving them. Then I go into the storeroom where we keep the can food and the wine and I get my suit coat from the hanger. I put on my suit coat and I check myself in the glass on the swinging door. Then I am ready to go to open up the place for the night.

"Are you ready?" I ask my brother.

"I am ready half an hour," Primo says.

Maybe here I should say a little bit about what our restaurant is like. We call it the "Paradise." When we first come to this country, we called it in Italian, *Il Paradiso,* like the name of the famous poem by Dante we read when we were kids in school. I like how this name sound. But then I think our customers want more to go to a restaurant with a name in English. Primo did not like to change the name to English, but I tell him it is good for the business, it makes the customers feel more comfortable.

A few months ago I got for us a new neon sign that says "Paradise" in red letters. It cost money we don't have, but I think we must do something to make the business come up. After we hang up the sign on top of the old painted one, I

told Primo to please come out and look. We stood in front
and watched when Cristiano threw the switch, and the sign
began to blink on and off, on and off.

I like this neon sign. It is very bright and it is like the
one Pascal have at his restaurant across the street, except
that he have three different signs on his place. But at least
this is a good start.

"What do you think?" I asked Primo after the sign blink
for awhile. "Now everybody can see us."

"Probably from all over the world," Primo said, and he
went back inside the restaurant. He does not understand
why I want to have this sign. Sometimes I think he likes to
be a pain in the neck just so he can be a pain in the neck.

Our dining room in the Paradise is not too big, not too
small. We have just a dozen tables and two banquettes. I like
the tables to be very simple—they have only white tablecloths and sometimes we put bud flowers on them that
Primo goes to get at the flower shop. We have chairs made
from bent wood and we have only stainless steel tableware,
and thick white dishes, nothing too fancy. This is the style of
the *trattoria* in Italy. The *trattoria* is a small kind of restaurant
that is run by the family and have the family's recipes for the
menu. Many *trattorie* are very old and have the same family
run them for generations, like our uncle's place.

Every night before we open I go through the whole restaurant and I check the tables and make sure Cristiano set
them the right way. I straighten them and I make sure they
are not shifty. When they wobble, I put a matchbook under
the leg to make it safe. I learn this trick from my Uncle
Paolo.

On the walls of the Paradise we have many paintings
and drawings—landscapes, portraits, sketches. Some we
bring from our home in Italy, and some we get from artists
we know here. I like to have this art on the walls because me

and brother both love to look at art. Our father liked to paint, and our aunt, but they worked so hard in Italy they never had much time to paint.

Some of our paintings come from Stash, a painter who likes to eat here and talk to Primo. Stash comes from Romania and he has been around in Europe, in Paris and Rome, so he knows what good food is and he eats whatever Primo makes for him. He will even eat a rabbit but we don't serve this to our regular customers yet because nobody here understands that rabbit taste just like chicken. When it is cooked like Primo make it, with a little tomato and red wine, a rabbit is delicious. But here people think it is wrong to eat a rabbit. In Italy, people have eaten rabbits for thousands of years. What is the big deal?

Because he is a painter, Stash doesn't have too much money, so he will give us a painting instead for his meal. My uncle does this with artists who come to his *trattoria* too. I don't mind this, but now we are starting to get too many paintings. Sometimes I think I should just open a museum and then maybe I can make money that way.

Near the front door of the restaurant we have a telephone booth and a small bar, and on the bar is a beautiful silver *macchina* that makes our *espresso* and *cappuccino*. We bring this machine from Italy, from our uncle's *trattoria* when he get a new one. I drink many *espressi* every day, and so does Primo. I do not like the coffee they make here in this country, it tastes like water to me, but we do serve it to our customers because they always want this American coffee. A cup of Joe, they say. I think this is funny to call coffee Joe but I still am learning everything about this country.

Before I open up the place every night at five o'clock I check the bar to make sure we have enough glasses, ice, beer and sometimes I like to take a shot of Scotch whisky for myself. This make me feel ready. Then I turn on the neon sign

and I turn around the little sign we have in the window that
say CLOSED to say OPEN and then I go and open the front door.

Sometimes when I open up I stand on the stoop of the
Paradise and I think how it will be when one day we have
many customers. I can see them coming up in their big cars,
their black Cadillacs, the beautiful girls laughing and smiling, all dressed up in their evening clothes, the handsome
men taking their arms and helping them out of the cars.
Everyone is happy and everyone is hungry to eat the food
we make, and there are so many people I have to turn some
away and tell them to come back tomorrow. They always say
they will come back. Our business is very good, and then
soon we must get a bigger place, bigger than Pascal's across
the street.

But tonight nobody is standing at the front of the restaurant when I go to open it up except me. This is how it is
every night. Sometimes I think we are not in the best location because we are down the hill from the main street of the
town toward the dock. Pascal have a better location because
he is on the corner of the main street and so everybody drive
by his place all the time. This is why I buy the neon sign so
people can see us from the main street. But still the business
is not so good. It is bad.

We come to this town in New Jersey because it is nearby
to New York City. It is called Northport and I like this place
because it is right near the ocean, very nice, very pretty. We
don't want to go to New York City because it is more expensive there and we can't afford to open our restaurant there
with the money we have. But we think because we are close
to the city we will get some people who love Italian food to
come here. And I see that Pascal does very well here so if he
can do it we can do it, too. In America there is room for
many people to do the same thing and everyone can make
money from it. It is not like Italy where there can be only

one or two places in a whole town. Here there is room for everybody who want to be a success to be one.

Everything is quiet on our street now and when I look down to the dock, I can see some boats are coming in from fishing in the ocean all day. The sun is just starting get lower in the sky and make the water look a little bit orange. I straighten up the flowerpots in front and look around the ground near the entrance. I kick a cigarette butt off the sidewalk. Everything is ready now to go, so I turn back inside and wait again for the customers to come.

"Wait! The *risotto!*"

I hold out the dish of seafood *risotto* to Primo and he sprinkles some parsley on. In my other hand I have the dish of *ziti con piselli.* He made this with peas from our garden in the back. It smells delicious like it always does.

Madonna miseria, why can't he hurry up? These customers have been waiting for half an hour already and they are hungry.

"Yes," he says and nods to me. "Go."

I give him a look and then I rush through the doors to the dining room.

"Oh, thank God," I hear the lady say when she see me come out with their food. "I'm just so hungry," she says to her husband.

They are our first customer to come in tonight in two hours. Stash is eating here again tonight and there is one other person, an old woman, who eats by herself. I think she is a sad woman, and she only comes because she thinks Primo is handsome and she likes to flirt with him. She always makes me go to get him from the kitchen to come out and say hello to her. She never leaves me a good tip but at least she comes back a few times.

When this man and lady come in I can tell that they are not sure about eating in our place because hardly anyone else is in here. But I make them very welcome right away. I take the lady's coat and I make them their drinks. The man ask for a highball and the lady ask for a grasshopper. I don't know what is this drink, a grasshopper, so she has to tell me. It is a green drink you make with creme de menthe. I think it look horrible, but it seems like she likes it and they start to relax a little bit. I think they like the paintings on the wall because they ask me who make this one and that one.

I know this lady and this man are very hungry waiting for Primo to make the *risotto*. If you ever try to cook *risotto* for yourself, you know it takes a long time. You have to add the broth a little bit at a time to the rice and keep stirring all the time. It is very hard work and you have to know just when the rice is *al dente* without cooking it too much. And you have to have the patience to stand at the stove for a long while. I don't like to make *risotto* because I never have the patience. But the *risotto* is one of the best dish my brother makes.

I serve the *signore* his pasta with the peas. He picks up the piece of basil Primo put on the plate for a garnish and he looks at it.

"Oh that looks good, you got leaves with yours," the lady says to him. She have the kind of low voice I do not like in a woman and her hair is big and all stiff from hair spray.

Cristiano stands next to me and helps me to serve the *risotto*. He holds the platter as I spoon it in a mound on the lady's plate. Then I flatten out the top of the mound.

"There you are, *signora*," I say. "You would like fresh pepper or cheese?"

"Cheese, lots of cheese," the man say, but the lady say, "No, I don't eat cheese," and I know already there is a big problem because in the *risotto,* of course, there is *parmigiano* cheese.

But I say nothing about this and I start to grate the fresh cheese onto the man's dish of pasta. The lady pokes at the *risotto* with her fork like it is a dead thing and she looks up at me and she says, *"Monsieur?* Is this what I ordered?"

"Yes," I say, "that is the *risotto.* It is a special recipe my brother and I bring from Italy. Delicious, I promise."

The lady makes a face and she says, "Well, it took so long I thought you went all the way back to Italy to get it," and she laughs. She think she is funny, this lady, so I have to laugh at her little joke.

"Yes, but is worth it, I promise," I say and I keep grating the cheese.

"I thought you said it would be rice with seafood," the lady says and she pokes at her *risotto* again. I stop with the cheese.

"Yes, it is Italian *arborio* rice, the best," I explain to her. "And then with shrimp, scallop . . ." Then the man touch my arm to tell me he wants more cheese, so I start to grate more on his plate.

"Well, I just don't see anything that looks like a shrimp or a scallop," she says, pushing the *risotto* around with her fork. She can't seem them because when you make seafood *risotto* you cut up the shrimp and scallop and they are white and the *arborio* is white.

Her husband gives her a look like to say, *Why are you making a problem?*

"I'm sorry," she says to him, "it just isn't what I expected."

I look at Cristiano. He has heard this before about the *risotto.* Then the man taps my arm. He wants even more cheese! *Che pazzo!*

"But I get a side order of spaghetti with this, right?" the lady asks.

"Why?" I say, and then I catch myself, and I say, "I mean, no."

Mr. Cheese waves his hand to say he finally has enough cheese, so I stop grating, and he says to me, "But I thought all the main courses come with spaghetti."

"Well, some, yes," I say, "but you see, *risotto* is rice, so it is a starch, and it doesn't go really with pasta." From the corner of my eye, I can see Stash looking over here. He probably thinks this to be funny. These people just don't understand.

"Well, I don't want pasta, I just want spaghetti," she says.

"So order a side of spaghetti," the man says to her. "And I'll eat your meatballs, honey."

"Yeah, he'll have the meatballs," the lady says, looking at me now with more hope in her eyes.

Meatballs. Spaghetti and meatballs, everyone always wants spaghetti and meatballs. I look at Cristiano again. He's heard this before, too.

"Well, the spaghetti comes without meatballs," I say to the lady and now she is confused like crazy. She look at me like I am telling her that I am the President of America.

"There are no *meatballs* with the *spaghetti?*" she asks and she looks at her husband, who looks at me.

"No," I say, "sometimes the spaghetti likes to be alone." I laugh at this, but she doesn't think this joke is very funny and she starts to smash the *risotto* with her fork and she says, "Well, then, we'll just have a side order of meatballs."

But now her husband says he does not want the meatballs and he just wants to eat, so they order a side order of spaghetti without the meatballs. She wants to know if *this* will take a long time, but I promise her that it will take only two minutes for her. But when I look at Cristiano he look at me like he is afraid because he know now what I have to do.

Primo looks at me with his face like a stone. His mustache is not moving at all. He is stirring in a pot and he never misses a stroke.

"Primo, please," I say. "Just c'mon."

"I want to know for who."

I should know this is going to happen. This always happen with him. I can't just come into the kitchen and ask him for something I need. It has to be a big deal. And this lady does not want to wait for her spaghetti.

"C'mon, just make me a side order of spaghetti," I say.

"Secondo, I want to know for who is it for," he says.

Cristiano comes in and he goes to the corner. He is chopping some onion for Primo but I think he just wants a good seat at the fights, if you know what I say.

I sigh and say, "For the lady with the *risotto*."

Primo bangs down the spoon in the pot.

"What?" he says. "Why?"

"She like starch, I don't know!" I say. "C'mon!"

"BITCH!" Primo barks out. *Madonna miseria*, he is starting again. This is just one side order of spaghetti, this is not World War III. But Primo starts to walk up and down like he is an animal in a cage and then he starts to talk to himself. I think he is a crazy person sometimes and right now I don't have time to wait for him.

"Okay, I make it myself!" I say and I try to go behind the stove. But he holds up his arm and he blocks me.

"Who are these people in America?" he says to me. "I want to talk to her."

"Oh, go on, please," I say. "What are you going to do, tell her what she can eat?" He is here in his kitchen and he is safe away from the customers. He doesn't know what I have to do with them out there. He thinks it is so simple.

"That is what she ask for!" I say and now I am getting very mad. "That is what the customer want! Make it! Make the pasta! Make it, make it, make it! C'mon, let's go!"

Primo looks at me like he is going to cry. "How can she want?" he says. "They both are starch! Maybe I should just make some mash potato for on the other side!"

I can't do this every fucking night. I go up very close to him and I think maybe if he can see why I need him to make this pasta right now he will give in. I say to him, "Primo, look, don't, okay? They are the first customer to come in two hour, the fucking pipes are broken —"

"NO!" he yells. "She is a criminal! I want to talk to her!" He walks away from me to behind the stove and he folds his arms. He makes it clear he is not making this pasta. Okay. Okay, now I want to kill him. I go up to him and point my finger right in his face.

"You want to talk to her?" I say. "I'm sick of this, every fucking night. You want to talk to her? Okay."

I walk past him to the swinging door that goes to the dining room and I kick it open. It makes a big bang sound but I don't care and I see the man and the lady turn around very fast and they look at us. Stash and the old woman look up at me too.

"GO! Go talk to her!" I yell at him.

I hold the door for a second and then I let go of the door and it starts to swing back and forth. The lady looks at Primo and he looks at the lady. She looks afraid some from what she hears us say in the kitchen. Primo just stands there and then he looks down at his shoes like he is thinking and the door stops swinging.

"No, she is a Philistine, I'm no gonna talk to her," he

says, waving his hand at the door. "She no understand anyway."

I glare at him. He has to torture me like this in front of the customers. And then I wonder why our business is no good. But at least I win. I go through the swinging doors to the dining room. The man and the lady look up at me when I come in. I just smile at them. They look very concerned. "It will be just a moment," I say to the lady in a very calm voice. "Is everything all right?"

"Oh, yes," the woman says like she is afraid to say that anything is bad because she doesn't know what could happen now. I get them some more bread and they start to look more calm down and then we all jump like rabbits when we hear the crash of something very loud against the swinging doors. Primo has thrown another pot. I smile at the man and the lady.

"Would you please excuse me for a moment?" I say and I head to go back into the kitchen. I always have to go back in.

When we go to bed in our room where we live above the Paradise, Primo goes to sleep very easy, but I stay awake in the night and think about what to do about the business. We do not have much money left, but I do not tell him this. My brother does not know the first thing to do with money, about what it is like to run the business. All he wants is to stay in his kitchen and cook his food. I think maybe he knows more about it than he says to me, but I don't think he knows we are in serious trouble with money right now.

But I don't want to tell him about this because there is no reason for him to get worried about it too. One of us to worry is enough. I am the one who is taking care of the business, so it is up to me to make sure we do okay.

Big Night

I have a letter I get from Mr. Pierce. He is the man at the bank who gave us the mortgage loan when we come to America. The letter say I am behind in the payment to the bank and I have to come in and talk to him about this. I know I am behind, this is no surprise to me, but I think if I wait a little bit and we get some more business, we can catch up with the payment. But now I think it is the bank that catch up with me instead.

My girlfriend Phyllis works at the same bank where Mr. Pierce work. She is a bank teller there and this is where I met her for the first time. One day about a year ago I go on her line with my deposit and I see that she is very beautiful. She has long red hair which is a kind of hair I always like and she have a very nice smile. So every time when I go back to the bank I stand on her line even if it is the longest line. After a while I can see that she likes me to be in her line. She knows I run the Paradise and she always asks me how the business is coming. I tell her business is getting better, even when it is not because I want to make her think I am a good restaurateur. Although I'm sure she can tell from the sad deposits I make that I am not exactly a millionaire.

One day when there is hardly anybody in the bank I ask her if she can go to have a drink with me after work. She says she gets off at three o'clock and that is much too early for her to have a drink. But I can tell she wants to, she is just making hard to get. But then her boss comes by and she has to stop talking to me and she writes something down on a paper and she says, "Thank you very much, sir, please come again," and I bow at her and leave. Outside I read the paper and on it she writes she will come by the Paradise that night and she did and we go together since then.

Phyllis knows the loan officer, this Mr. Pierce, at the bank a little bit and she says he is a tough customer. I know what she means when she says this, tough customer. I think all the customer we have are tough customer. She says Mr. Pierce is a very serious man and she tries to be nice to him because she hopes he will help us out. But she has to be careful because of her job. She can't get too much in the middle of things and of course I understand this.

When I come into the bank in the morning, she looks at me from behind the cage where she works. She knows I am here to meet Mr. Pierce and she looks worried for me. I don't stop to talk to her because I know she is working so I just look at her and go right over to Mr. Pierce's office. It is near the back of the bank near the big vault where they keep all the money.

Mr. Pierce is a tall and skinny man who is probably about forty years old and he is losing his hair. He asks me if I want to have a cigarette so I take one, and then he tells me to sit down across from his big desk. His office looks different, like they have fixed it all up since I was here when I signed the loan two years ago.

"So this looks completely different," I say. "It's a beautiful renovation."

"Yes," he says, "we're very happy with it."

"Yes," I say. "Because you know we went through that with our restaurant when we first come here, very difficult."

"It's a lot of money, a lot of work," he says, looking around him.

"Yes, a real pain in the neck, you know?" I say. I cross my legs and I try to look relaxed. I want him to know I am in control of the business, that he can trust me. "But I think it come out okay. Because it is a simple place, you know, casual, for the family to come."

On his desk I see he has a photograph of him with his wife and his two kids and I think to myself maybe if he would come to eat and taste what Primo cook, bring his family for dinner, no charge, he will give to me a break for paying the loan.

"You like Italian food?" I ask him.

"I do, very much," he says, "but I'm going to have to change the direction of this conversation right now." He goes right down to the point, this Mr. Pierce, like Phyllis says.

"Sure, I understand," I say.

He opens up a ledger and looks at the numbers. I smoke my cigarette and it tastes rough and bitter. Is hot in this bank today and my suit feel scratchy.

Mr. Pierce looks up at me and he is not smiling. "Is there someone you can borrow from?" he asks. "Back in . . . back home?"

"Well, no," I tell him. "You see, we did that already, to come here, so . . ."

"I see," he say.

To come here we use some money we have left from when our father die and we borrow some money from my Uncle Paolo and my Uncle Marco. I can't ask them for any more now. I have already ask them for too much, and now we are here I think we have to make money on our own.

Mr. Pierce asks, "Do you have any salable assets?"

I try to think of what we can sell. "Well, uh, I don't know," I say.

"Something to sell," he says. "Like a car. For money. To pay us."

"Yes, yes, I understand you."

"Oh, well, I wasn't sure —"

"I speak English," I say. These people always think that because I talk with an accent I don't understand what they say. I do understand English. I learn it in school. I don't know how to say everything exactly right all the time, but I

pick it up very easy because I get around a lot for the business. I think my English is pretty good. Primo never learns
very good English and since we come here he doesn't go out
like I do. He stays home to read or listen to opera or he goes
over to Alberto's barbershop on our street and he talks Italian with Alberto.

I am thinking of what I can sell. I can't sell my car. Is a
big piece of shit, but it is the only car I have. "I have a car,
yes, but is no Cadillac," I say to Mr. Pierce. "And I need my
car, for the business."

"I see," Mr. Pierce says and he makes a frown.

"I don't know, maybe something else," I say even though
I know there is nothing else.

He sits back in his chair. "Well, I don't know what to
say," he tells me. "Your payments over the past two years
have hardly been consistent."

"Yes, I know," I say.

I pay as much as I can whenever I can but he already
knows this so I say nothing else. Then Mr. Pierce is very
quiet for a long time. It seems like an hour. I know what he
is going to say. I try to think of something to say, and then
Mr. Pierce looks up at me.

"I'm afraid we can't give you any more time," he says.

"What do you mean?"

He repeats what he said and then he closes the ledger.

"Okay, look, Mr. Pierce," I say. "Let me explain something to you. I am doing everything I can, but my situation
is unusual."

I want to explain about Primo and why it has taken us
so long to get our business going.

"My brother," I say, "he is . . . you see, when we came
here —"

"Look, I hate to see businesses fail," I hear Mr. Pierce
say.

"We work very hard," I say, "I mean, we are not lazy—"

"Look, I hate to see businesses fail, I really do," he says louder this time. He wants me to stop talking.

"So do I," I say.

"But we're a bank," he says. "We can't help people who can't help themselves. I'd love to give you some friendly advice, but I don't know anything about the restaurant business. I go to them, to eat."

Then he looks at me very serious and he says, "If we don't receive your payment by the end of the month, we will foreclose."

I know what this means. Good-bye Paradise. Everything we work for so far, gone. I do not know what to say to him, so I say, "I understand."

He stands up and I guess this means the talk is done. So I get up from the chair and he puts out his hand and I shake his hand.

"Thank you very much," I say and he says, "Sure."

Sure for him. Not too sure for me.

Chapter Two

Basic Risotto

Bring about 5 cups of meat or chicken broth to a simmer on a stove. (It is best to use homemade broth, but you can substitute 1 cup canned chicken broth mixed with 4 cups of water.) Finely chop 2 tablespoons of shallot or onion. In a heavy-bottomed pan, sauté the onion over medium-high heat with 2 tablespoons of butter and 1 tablespoon of olive oil until the onion is translucent.

Add 1½ cups of Italian *arborio* rice to the pan and stir until it is well coated. (You cannot use American-style rice to make *risotto*.) Sauté for a minute, then add ½ cup of the simmering broth. Gently stir the rice until it absorbs all the liquid, then add another ½ cup of broth and continue stirring. Continue adding broth and stirring for about 20 minutes. Never flood the rice with broth; it must absorb the liquid gradually.

Don't set the heat level too high—risotto is not boiled rice—nor too low, which will make the rice pasty. After about 20 minutes, taste the rice. It should be tender, but firm to the bite. If it is still too firm, add more broth in ¼-cup intervals until it is done. (If you run out of broth, use simmering water.)

When the rice is just about done, add 1½ cups of freshly grated *parmigiano* cheese and mix well. Taste for salt and add some fresh pepper if you like. Serve immediately with more grated cheese on the side. Serves 4 people.

Primo

"I wish I could pay you with money," Stash say to me.

"Money, what would I do with money?" I tell him.

Stash bring us a new painting tonight to pay for his dinner. He tell me he think he is start a whole new kind of painting for him, something he never do before. He is very excite about this. Is the abstract kind of painting, just color and line and shape.

I like it when Stash come by because he always like what I make for him to eat. He like to eat a lot. He know good food because he is not from this country. Before he come here, he live in Paris and other place and he study how to paint.

We always sit in the booth and have a *caffè* when the night is done. He like to tell me stories about when he grow up in Romania and I tell him about Italia, about my uncle and our life in the *trattoria*. I think he like being in America more than in Romania because his country is very poor and have many bad politics that are no good for the artist to do his work. He like that in this country at least you can be free to do what it is you want, you can make your art and nobody can come to arrest you. This can be true, I say to him, but what good is this if nobody understand what it is you try to do?

When we talk Seco is stand behind the bar and he is count the money we make for this week. We no have too many customer this week. I see that we no have many customer come in lately. One night last week it rain very hard and nobody come in here at all. Tonight Stash is the only one who come in but I no like to make Stash pay because he is our friend and he give us his painting. It is a big canvas roll.

Stash get up from the booth and he go over to Secondo to say good night to him.

"How was everything, Stash?" Seco ask him.

"Oh, unbelievable, thank you, Secondo," Stash say. "No one else around here serve rabbit." I make a rabbit stew tonight but I think it no come out too good. It is too dry.

"Was it dry?" I ask Stash.

"Dry? No, it was moist," Stash say and he close his eyes. "Like the lips of a young girl."

Seco laugh at this. He is a funny man sometime, Stash.

Stash say to Seco, "I wish I could give you money, but . . ."

"That's okay," Seco say to him. "Someday, Stash, you'll be a rich and famous artist and then you pay me with money."

My brother no have to say this to Stash. This is an insult to Stash. I give Seco a look but he ignore me. Stash just laugh at what Secondo say and say nothing.

"Well, good night," Stash say to us and he leave. I roll down the canvas that Stash give me and inside there is a colorful painting, very beautiful. I ask Stash what he call it and he say it have no title but is a landscape.

"Look, you see what he give us?" I say to Seco. "It's a landscape. Don't you love it?"

Seco hardly look at the painting. "Great," he say and he roll his eye at me. "Put it with the rest of them." He point to the stack of canvases from Stash we have behind the bar.

Sometime I think that all Seco care about is the money. He always look worry when he count the money. I can see that we no have so many customer like we should have but he worry too much about this. I know what I cook some people never see before. This food is strange to them. They only know the kind of food they have in the restaurants they call Italian in this country.

But most of these restaurants are run by people who come only from Sicily or from Napoli. They have lots of heavy tomato sauce on their pasta and on everything and this is only one kind of cooking from Italy. They do not serve all the dishes from all the region of Italia. There are many different kind of food in all the place all over my country. Every place have its own kind of cooking. My uncle travel around very much in Italia and he learn different foods from Emilia-Romagna, from the Veneto, from Lombardy, from all the region, and he teach us how to cook these.

So I know our customer will take some time to understand what I make. I no think Seco like this because he want to make money here. He want to be a big success. I say he can be one but he have to wait some time, he must have some patience. But he see the money that is here in this country and he think to have it right away.

I miss my country very much and I miss my family very much. But at least I can talk to Alberto next door to us. He is a barber and he come to here from Italy many year ago but is like he still live in the old country. His English never get to be good and he is fine with this. I think I don't have to learn English either. Who do I need to talk English to be in my own kitchen? Only Cristiano is there with me and he don't speak so good English anyway.

Also at least I can get the *Il Progresso* newspaper here that they write in Italian and I can know what is happen in my country. We are done for tonight so I get my paper and a glass of Sambuca and I go to read in the booth in the corner. Secondo is still work on the books.

"Primo, let me ask you something," my brother say to me. "How do you feel if we take *risotto* off the menu?"

I hear him say this but I say nothing. There is nothing for me to say to this. This is not even a idea to talk about. I look at the story about *il calcio*.

"Primo, what do you think about that?" he say. "Take *risotto* off the menu."

I look up from my newspaper and I say, "I'm sorry, what did you say?" and he know I no want to talk about this.

"Forget it," he say like he is mad with me and then go back to his money. Cristiano come in with a tray of clean glasses for the bar and I see Seco hand to him his pay for the week.

"No, I no hear what you say," I say to Seco. "Tell me what you say."

Seco put out his cigarette and he get that look in his face that say he want to say something serious to me. "Well, it's just that *risotto* costs us a lot," he say. "And it take you a long time to make. I mean, you must work so hard to make, so, then we have to charge more, and these customers don't understand really what is a *risotto*. And so there always is a problem."

I say nothing for a second. He want to change everything. He want to make our restaurant like all the other restaurant and then we can have more customer. He put up a flash sign like Pascal have, it is so bright. He want me to make meatball. He no understand anything. Every time I must explain everything to him. I think sometimes this is because he is my little brother. He need someone to teach him how to do everything right.

But I say nothing except, "Sure, good."

"Really?" he say. He look surprise that I am agree with him and he turn back to his money. "Okay, *grazie*," he say and he go back to his money. I put down my newspaper and sip some of my Sambuca. Now I think is a time to teach him a good lesson.

"Maybe instead we could put—" I say.

"Yes, tell me, tell me," he say and he come from behind the bar with his stack of money. He sit down across from me in the booth.

"I was thinking . . . uh . . . what do they call them?" I say. "You know." I hold my hands out in front of me to show him the shape I think of. I make a long and thin shape.

"*Manicotti?*" he say.

"No, no, you know," I say. "*Come si dice?* Hot dog? Yes, hot dog. Hot dogs!" I look down at my newspaper and I say, "I think people would like that. Those."

I feel he is mad because he close his eyes to me. "Fine," he say.

"If you give people time, they learn," I say to him.

"Well, I don't have time for them to learn," he say and he pick up the stack of money. "This is a restaurant, not a fucking school!"

He get up and he walk away from me. I know he understand what I mean to say but I know also that he still want the money first. He have to have some patience. But he have no patience, my brother. He want everything fast, fast, fast.

After I read the newspaper for a little bit I go and I finish clean up the kitchen with Cristiano and tell him to go home. Then I change my shirt to go over to see Alberto like I do every night. When I go outside in the front Seco is out there with a cigarette. He change his clothes too and I can see he is probably go out again somewhere.

The air is very warm and nice outside and there is music come from Pascal's restaurant across the street and up a little bit from the Paradise. He call his place "Pascal's Italian Grotto" but I no see a grotto anywhere around here. His restaurant is busy all the time. I know Seco sometimes come out here and watch the customer come and go in Pascal's and it make him crazy. He wish we have this many people in our place. Cars pull up in front, one, then another, then another. Everybody is always laugh and look like they have a good time over there. I no understand how they can do this when Pascal's food is like what a dog will no eat. This is a mystery to me. How can they like this food?

I take Seco's cigarette from his mouth and I light mine with his. We both look over and watch Pascal's.

"He's busy again tonight," Seco say and look at me.

"The man should be in a prison for the food he serve," I say.

Seco make a big sigh. "People love it," he say to me.

I look at him. I know what he is try to say to me here. He know it make no difference to me if people love it but I know him. He want to make me think again about the *risotto* and that we should take it off the menu.

"Look, Primo," he say, "I am only trying to make things more easy."

Yes, and this is why he always get himself in trouble. Because he try to go easy, to make things more easy. Sometimes though you can't make things easy. You can't cook the *risotto* easy. There is only one way and that is the hard way.

"Easy," I say to him. "What is easy for you is not always what is good for you."

Seco sigh again and throw down his cigarette. I know he still is mad but I no care right now. He is stubborn and he need to learn. He start to walk away from me.

"Good night," he say.

"Where do you go?" I say.

"To see Phyllis."

"Oh," I say, "say hi for me." It is good he go to see his girlfriend Phyllis. I like Phyllis very much.

"Okay," he say and he start to walk away from me again.

"You go out?" I say. He stop and turn around to me.
"Yes."
"Where?"
"Out," he say, "to a movie."
I look down the street to the dock. There are some lights
there but is so dark the water look black. Sometime I think
about how the Atlantic Ocean can be so big and how long
away it is to Italy where I come from. When we come over
on the ship two year ago it seem like we will never get here.
"Do you want to come with us?" he say.
"Why?" I say. "No, I go see Alberto."
"Okay," he say. "Good night." He start to walk again to
his car and I call out to him, "What is the movie?"
I don't know why I say this. I don't even like to go to the
movie very much. It is usually too loud for me and there are
too many people. I guess I just want to know where he go.
"Do you want to come?" he say. "C'mon."
"No, no," I say.
He come back to me. "C'mon, call up the flower lady,"
he say. "*Come si chiama?* What's her name, Ann? Ann, right?
Double date."
I look down the street again. "Who? Why would I call
her?" I say but I don't look at him. Of course I know who
he mean. Ann is a woman who own the flower shop I go to
buy the flower for our table. I like to go there because I like
to see the flower and I like to see her. She is a widow and
she is very nice to me.
Seco say, "I don't know, Alberto said that you and she
were . . ." and he smile at me.
"What?" I say.
"You know."
"He said that?" I say.
"Yeah, it's no secret," he say. "It takes you longer each
time when you go to buy the flowers."

"Well, I don't grab just any flower," I say, "I like to pick the right one." I take a smoke of my cigarette and I look down at the ocean water again.

"Well, don't take too long," Seco say to me and he brush a piece of tobacco off my shirt. "Someone else might pick the one you want." He think he is so funny. But what he say make me smile and Seco laugh a little bit.

"*Ciao,*" he call to me as he walk away.

"*Ciao,*" I say.

He go to the car and he drive away. I know he just like to tease me about Ann but I don't like it when he and Alberto talk about me on the behind of my back. I will say something to Alberto when I go to see him later. First I want to make a phone call. I finish my cigarette and I watch Pascal's for another minute and then I go back inside.

I sit in the phone booth and I pick up the phone and dial for the phone operator. "I want Italy," I say to her. She say to hold the line so I can talk to the other one, the overseas operator.

When the other one come on I say, "Hello, operator, I can call Italy?" and I give her the phone number of my aunt and uncle in Frascati. I know it is late in Italy because is six hour ahead of here but I want to talk to them so much. The overseas operator say she will call me back when she have my uncle on the line.

I call Italy every month on the telephone even though Secondo say it cost us a lot. Sometime there is a lot of static and I can hardly hear what my uncle say. While I wait I have another glass of Sambuca from the bar and I smoke a cigarette and I read some more of the *Il Progresso* newspaper. Is very quiet here in the Paradise when no one is here but myself. I like this quiet but sometimes I feel very sad when I think too much about my home.

The phone ring and I answer and say to the operator I am here. Then I wait a bit and then my Aunt Maria come on the line. I am so happy to hear her voice! She ask me how I am and she make me laugh because every time I talk to her she always ask me the same thing, what the weather is like here and what time is it here. Then she put my Uncle Paolo on the phone.

When our father die, Secondo and me go to live with my Uncle Paolo and Aunt Maria above his *trattoria* in Frascati. This is a town just on the outside of Roma up on a hill and you can see all of the city spread out from there. Our mother die when we are just only little boy and she is got very sick with a fever. I don't remember her too much just that she is beautiful. And I can remember her voice a little bit. We have only one photo of her with my father on the day when they get marry. She is very tall and she have curly black hair and I think she look more like me than she look like my brother.

Our father raise us up with our *nonna* after our mother die. But when I am nine year old and Seco is six our father get sick, too. One winter he get *la polmonite,* or like they call it in this country, the pneumonia, and he just never get better from this. So our Uncle Paolo, who is the brother of our father, take us to his house to live. We have to help him in his *trattoria* and *Zio* Paolo teach us what we know about cooking, how to serve the customer, everything. I think he is a *maestro* in the kitchen.

When *zio mio* come on the phone I tell him we don't do so well here in America. The customer are very slow to come in and then they have problem with the food I make because they want spaghetti and meatball all the time. He laugh at this, spaghetti and meatball, but I tell him this is not funny because Seco say we need to have more customer and he want me to make meatball all the time. Uncle Paolo can't believe what I tell him.

I know I can't talk to him for very much time because the phone to Italy cost a lot. He tell me he think to open a new restaurant right inside the city of Roma and that he already write me a letter that tell me all about it. I no want to say good-bye to him but I do and I tell him to say hello to everyone there for me and that I miss them all very much.

When I hang up I sit in the phone booth for a minute. It seem like he is just here, Uncle Paolo, and now he is gone already.

I go to the kitchen to get some of the rabbit stew, a *cacciatora*, I make to bring to Alberto. This is a recipe my uncle get from his grandmother and is very old. It is a rabbit you marinate in lemon and herbs and olive oil and then you cook with tomato and red peppers. But I think I cook it this time too long and I let it get dry. I know I should just throw it out but I think maybe Alberto will like.

I go see Alberto every day and I like to bring him and his wife Ida food I make but no customer eat. We have a *caffè* and talk about Italia and my brother and everything. Alberto is around seventy year old. He is a short man but strong like a bull and what I like about him the most is he is very calm. It take a lot to make him get mad. Even Ida who I think is a little crazy and talk a lot and even scream at him sometime can't make him too upset. He just do what he like to do. He take care of his customer and everyone who come in his shop like him. I think this is because he don't talk too much when he cut the hair. He let the customer talk. He is very smart, Alberto.

"*Buona notte, maestro,*" he say at the door when I knock for him. He like to call me *maestro*.

"*Ciao,*" I say.

"How was tonight?"

"Please," I say and I show him the pot I carry. "Here, I bring you the special. Rabbit. It might be a little dry, so if you no like, throw it out."

"Come in, come in," he say and he take the pot from me. Inside Alberto's barber shop it smell like hair tonic and after-shave and it is very clean. He have two old brown leather barber chair in the middle. I think these are the same chair he get when he open his shop forty year ago. I sit in one of the chair and I spin it around and look at myself in the mirror.

"What did you say to my brother?" I ask him.

"About what?"

"Where's Ida?" I ask him.

"Ida's sleeping," he say. I stop the spin and I get up from the chair and go over to the table he have in the corner. He sit here and read his newspaper and sometime he play cards with other men from the town.

"About the flower lady," I say.

"Who? The widow?" he say. "Ann?"

"Yes, Ann, Ann." He know who I mean.

"I said nothing," he say and he start to make himself busy with the radio.

"Oh," I say. "He said you said something."

Alberto shrug at me. "I may have mentioned her," he say. "But I didn't say anything. What the matter with you?"

I just grunt at him. I know he say something to Seco and he no want to tell me. I want to know what they say about me when I am not there.

"You want a drink?" he say and he take down a bottle of *grappa* from the shelf where he keep his cards. "Have a little drink, it'll make you feel better."

I sit down at the table with him. His radio play some nice music from the Italian radio station, a kind of folk song I think. Alberto pour me a drink and one for himself and then we toast with *salute* and drink.

"Where's your brother?" he ask me.

"He's out wandering," I say. "He's a wanderer."

I know what he is try to do. He is like my brother. He try to make me think about something else. But I no let him get away from this so easy.

"How come you say you say nothing when Seco say you say something?" I ask him.

"Primo," Alberto say. "I am like the monkey. I don't see, I don't hear, and I don't speak. *Ecco.*"

"Listen," I say. "If you want to talk about Ann, talk to me. Not to my brother."

"Sure, sure, whatever you say," he say and pour some more *grappa*. "Whatever you want."

But I know he just say this to make me shut up. I know he and Seco will talk about me and Ann. But this is stupid. Me and Ann, me and Ann. There is no me and Ann anyway, so they are waste their time to talk.

"Let's see what you brought tonight," he say and he take the lid from off the pot. He taste the rabbit *cacciatora* I make.

"Mmmm, *che buono!*" he say. "Delicious."

"It might be a little dry," I say. This is what happen when you cook too long. The rabbit get tough.

Alberto look at me very serious and then he taste the rabbit again. "You know, you're right," he say, "it is a little dry." But then he smile and start to laugh. He is only make a joke with me. This make me laugh and he toast with me again and we drink our *grappa*. Now, at least for now, when I am sit here with Alberto, I am feel better.

Chapter Three

Pascal's Meatballs

Polpette ∂i Carne ∂i Pascal

In a large bowl, combine 1½ pounds of ground beef; ¼ cup each of dried bread crumbs, grated Parmesan cheese, finely chopped onion, and milk; a slightly beaten egg; 2 tablespoons chopped parsley; 1 teaspoon salt; ½ teaspoon dried oregano; and a dash of black pepper. Mix thoroughly, and using your hands, firmly shape into 1-inch meatballs.

Heat a good quantity of vegetable oil in a large skillet that has a cover. When the oil is hot, slide the meatballs in with a spatula and brown on all sides. Turn them carefully so they don't break up or stick to the pan. (You can cook them in batches, but it's better to use a big pan that will accommodate them all at once.) When they're done, remove the meatballs to drain on paper towels.

Tip the pan and spoon off the excess fat. Put all the meatballs back into the pan and add 1½ cups of canned Italian tomatoes and their juice, and a pinch of salt. Cover and cook for 25 minutes, turning the meatballs occasionally, until the tomato has thickened into a sauce. Serves 6 people.

Secondo

Phyllis and me go to watch a movie at the movie house in the town. This movie is called *Written on the Wind* and is about this rich family in Texas that has oil wells and lots of money but nobody is very happy. The son hates the father and he is a drunk. It seems like it is a pretty good movie, but I don't pay too much attention to it because I am thinking so much about the business. I can't sit still in my chair and I have to get up in the middle and go out. I ask Phyllis if she wants something but she just shakes her head and keeps on staring at the screen.

"Are you all right?" she whispers and I nod yes at her and she goes back to the movie.

Phyllis loves to go to the movies. She always wants me to take her. She says to me that sometimes she will go to see the same movie more than one time and she says she likes to cry when she watches the movies. A good cry, she calls this. I don't understand this. I know the movies are not real. The people in a movie always have big problems but it is just a movie. No one really is having a hard time and in the end everything usually works out good. I know that this is not what happens in real life.

When we were in the line to buy the tickets to the movie Phyllis talked to me about her job at the bank. She said she likes to work in the bank but her boss bothers her all the time.

"How long will it take him to trust me?" she said to me

and she pushed her hair back from her face. "He's always over my shoulder. I've been at that bank for three years, and not one cent has ever been wrong."

"Well, money makes people to act funny sometimes," I said.

"Yes, I know, Seco, but I mean, look at me," she said.

"Yes, I like to," I said. Tonight she is wearing a dark blue dress and pearls around her neck and she looks beautiful. She always looks beautiful.

"No, I mean, look into my eyes," she said. "Could I ever do anything like that? C'mon. If he can't trust me . . ."

"I know, Phyllis," I said, "you don't have to tell me."

I kissed her on the cheek and she smiled at me. When we reached the ticket lady, Phyllis told me she wanted to pay for the tickets.

"Why?" I said, but I know why.

"Because I want to," she said, and she started to open up her purse. She knows I am having trouble with the restaurant and she thinks she can help me. When I picked her up with the car she asked about my meeting with Mr. Pierce but I did not tell her everything. I just told her it was all going to work out with some time. But she can tell I am worried.

"No, no, no," I said when she started to take out money.

"Well, let's go dutch," she said.

"What do you mean?"

"Dutch," she said. "It's an expression. It means we'll split it. I pay for mine and you pay for yours."

"No, no," I said and I gave the lady the money. "No, I ask you to a movie. So I take you to a movie."

"Oh, all right," Phyllis said. "But I'll get the popcorn."

Now in the lobby of the movie house it is very quiet. I light a cigarette and stand by the window and look outside. It is raining a little bit and the street is very dark, very quiet.

I am thinking about Mr. Pierce and the money and what to do. I must do something to get more money for us. I try to push Primo to make food that is more like what people want but I know that this is not the only thing we can do. It is different in America and I see sometimes it is not even the food that people care about. They sometimes want something else.

I have to get money from someone. I think maybe I can ask Alberto but I know he doesn't have a lot of money to lend me. I think he just makes enough with his barbershop. I do not want to ask him anyway. He is too much our friend to ask for money.

I watch the boy behind the counter who sells the candy and the popcorn. He is just a kid. There is light all around this counter and the candy is very bright red and yellow and green. A fat lady with a big blue hat is by the counter and she is buying some popcorn in a paper bag. The kid takes the bag and he pours some melted butter into the bag and shakes it up. Then he puts on a lot of salt. When I see this red candy and this greasy popcorn I think maybe I do not understand at all what people like to eat in this country. How can they eat this?

When we leave the movie theater and we walk to the car Phyllis says, "Wasn't that great? It was so passionate."

"Sure," I say.

"What's the matter?" she says.

"Nothing," I say. "I think I just am tired."

Then Phyllis and me go "parking." This is a very American thing to me, this "parking," but Phyllis says that this is what couples in this country do when they are dating. We can't go to her house because her parents are there which is okay with me.

We are parking on a quiet street near the water and we get in the backseat of my car. We begin to kiss and I start to feel her body. I feel her long red hair and I smell her flower perfume between her breasts and I start to touch her back and kiss her neck. Her skin is so smooth. She holds my head in her hands when she kiss me but then I have to break away from her.

"What's wrong?" she asks.

"No, nothing," I say, "I just . . ."

"What?"

"No, I just," I say and I turn away from her. "I can't. I mean I don't want to."

"Oh," she says. I can hear in her voice that she is hurt by what I say.

"No, I mean I want to," I say, "but it drives me crazy."

"Well, good," she says and she smiles at me and she starts to kiss my face all over again. I start to kiss her again, and we kiss very hard, and I want to keep on kissing her, but then again I have to stop.

"No, Phyllis, I can't," I say. "I just get sad."

"Sad?"

"Yes."

"Honey, sad is the wrong word," she says, thinking that I don't have good English. She always tells me when I say the wrong word.

"No, not sad, I mean, but it gets me, you know, all jazzed up," I say, "and then I want to go only one place, but I can't go there. And then I have to go crazy."

Phyllis looks at me a little embarrassed by what I say and she stares down at her dress and smooths it out in front of her. I forget sometimes that she is really only a young girl, she is only twenty-four years old and she still has a lot to learn about how everything is in life.

"Well, we don't have to, we can . . . I mean, we've done other things," she says in a quiet voice and she smiles at me like a little girl smiles.

"No, I know," I say.

"So what's the problem?" she says, and she looks at me.

"Well, I just, for you and me to be something, okay," I say, not knowing what I want to say, because my mind is all mixed up. She thinks this is so easy, well, it's not so easy to say and I don't know if she can understand what I mean. I say, "Because these things are very important, you know, it's not for me, you know, just a casual thing."

"Well, it's not for me either," she says.

"I know, I just . . ." I say. "No. Because everything now is just too much and I want us to be something when I am more set."

"Set," she says.

"Yes."

"Oh," she says. Now I am making her annoyed. "So this is a question of finances."

"Well," I say, "no—"

"This is about money." She says the word like it is a bad curse.

"No, it's not about money, Phyllis," I say, "and don't say it like that, you know? Because here I am, I am working very hard, trying to do something here. And you know my brother is driving me crazy. And yes, okay, it is about money, I am sorry if you don't understand money."

"What?" she says and makes a short laugh. "I only work in a bank."

"What did you say?"

She stops smiling. "I understand money," she says.

"Oh," I say. "Good for you."

She looks out her window and sighs. I look out the window, too. The night is very dark and there is only one streetlight down the road. I can hear the crickets singing. They are very loud down here in this part of the town. I turn back to her and I lean close in.

"Honey," I say, quiet now, and I take her hand, "all I want is for the time to be right."

"I know," she says and she turns back to me and she looks at me like she loves me. I know she loves me. She is so beautiful.

I say, "And I want it to be right for you. Because now it is not right for you. Do you understand what I mean?"

I start to kiss her hand and up her arm, but I can feel her freeze up inside like an icebox, so I stop. There is silence and I can hear her breathing. She takes her arm away from me. What did I say now? She is a young girl and she doesn't understand what problems I have.

"You know," she says to the window, "I don't think you know what you want."

I don't know what she means by this. Of course I know what I want. I want to make the Paradise a success. I want Primo to stop driving me crazy. I want Phyllis not to push me right now. I have too many things to think about right now and I can't worry about it if the time is right with Phyllis or not.

"What do you want, Phyllis?" I say to her. "You know exactly what you want?" You want me to ask you to marry you right now?"

"Oh, is that a proposal?" She is angry at me now.

"Well, no," I say. "No."

She turns to me and she looks right into my eyes. "Do you want to marry me?" she says. Marry, marry, marry. That's all these American girls want. That's all they worry about.

"Do I want to marry you?" I say.

"Yes."

"Yes," I say to her. "Someday, probably, yes, in the future, I want to marry you, Phyllis, but not right now. Thank you very much, but not right now." Now I am the one who is annoyed. What does she want me to say?

"Okay," she says but she sounds like she might cry now. Part of her is happy because I say I want to marry her one day, but the other part is upset. I can see she is confused by what I say about getting married. To say the truth, so am I. But why do we have to talk about getting married right now? I am not ready to get married right now and that's it. I have to deal with the business, I have to get some money first.

"Honey, you know I love you so much," I say to her and I take her hand again.

"I know you do," she says, holding on to my hand. "But Seco, if you're worried about me, don't. I'm fine. I mean, if the restaurant doesn't . . . isn't . . . it doesn't matter. It just doesn't matter."

"Well, thank you," I say, "but to me it does matter."

"No, I didn't mean it that way," she says and then she sighs. "Look, just forget it."

"What?" I say.

"No," she says, "forget it."

We sit there a minute in the dark. I rub my eyes with my hands.

"I don't know," I say. She doesn't say anything. "I am so tired," I say.

"Yes," Phyllis says, "it's very late." And I know from the way she says this it is time to take her home.

I get out of the car and go to the front seat and start up the car. I look in the rearview mirror at her and she looks back at me very mad. But I don't care. I don't have time for this right now. After a minute she gets out of the car and gets in the front seat. But she turns away from me and on the ride to her house we don't say anything to each other.

Big Night

In front of her house, I get out of the car and go around it and open her door, but she gets out and walks right past me very fast without saying good night or anything. I watch her go up the sidewalk to the stoop and she goes into the house and then the porch light goes out. This is great. Like I don't have enough problems, I have to have a big fight with Phyllis.

When I get back to the Paradise I park my car in front and I look over at Pascal's restaurant. It is almost midnight now but there still are many people coming in and out as usual, laughing and talking. I think I know now what I maybe can do about the money, so I light a cigarette and walk over to Pascal's. It rained a little bit when we were in the movie and the streets are shiny with puddles of water. I have to watch where I walk so I don't get my shoes wet.

Leo, the doorman, is a big guy and he looks like some kind of animal, like a bear. He is always around Pascal, almost like he is a bodyguard. He is dressed in a tuxedo, very nice. I think he is a nice guy, Leo, but he is not too smart.

"Hey, how ya doin'?" he says when he sees me.

"Good, good," I say. "Is he here?"

"Yeah, I don't know, in the back," he says, and he opens the door for me.

When you go into Pascal's restaurant it is like going into a *carnevale*. First, there is lots of noise. Lots of people, and they are all talking very loud, and glasses and plates clanging and crashing and there is laughing, lots of laughing, and people are smoking away and drinking up a storm. In the corner of the room there is a girl singer in a shiny dress and a guy in a tuxedo playing the organ. She is singing *"O Sole Mio,"* which I'm sure you know is a famous Italian song, but I never heard anybody sing it like this before. It sounds more like a jazz song, but like the kind that you want to turn off when it come on the radio. The best thing you can say about this girl singer is she sings very loud.

Gabriella is at the front and she says *"Ciao"* to me. She looks very sexy like she always do. She is the hostess for the place and she is Pascal's girlfriend and that's not all she is. But right now I can't talk to her. She is busy with the customers and she picks up two menus and takes two to their table and I walk in behind them.

The way I would tell you how Pascal's look is that it is very red. *Tutto rosso.* The walls are red and the napkins and tablecloths are red and the lights from the little electric candles in the walls are red, too. He have very bad paintings of places in Italy on all the walls, like the canal in Venice and the Leaning Tower of Pisa. I think maybe it look a little like they say Hell look, except in here, it seems like everybody is having a good time.

I watch the waiters rush back and forth. They wear white shirts and black bow ties and red jackets. When I look at the dishes they are bringing out, they are spaghetti and meatballs, everywhere spaghetti and meatballs, and I see big plates of *antipasti* and I can see from one it look like everything come from out of a can. I know why Primo gets so mad about Pascal's food. Nothing looks like it is fresh to me and everything smells like too much garlic is in it. But the customers! They are eating everything up like it's going to fly off their plates.

Pascal's restaurant is much bigger than the Paradise. It has thirty tables and twenty booths and there are two rooms with a bar in the middle. When I walk to the bar, Gabriella starts to pass me on the way into the kitchen.

"Hello, how are you?" I say to her.

"Good, and you?" she says. She is all out of breath.

"Busy tonight, huh?"

She throws up her hand and says, "Friday night!" but she keeps on going into the kitchen. I can tell she don't want to talk to me right now. We both know that it is better that we don't talk too much to each other here, anyway, because of Pascal.

I go over to the bar where Charlie, the bartender, is making drinks. Charlie is a big man too, but a very friendly guy. I like Charlie. He always has a joke for me and he gives me a free drink, too.

"Hey, number two," he says. "You're here early. What's your poison?"

"Scotch a soda," I say. "Busy tonight, hey, Charlie?"

"Well, you know, Friday night," he says.

Then I look down to the end of the room and I see Pascal at a table that must have twenty people at it. Somebody is having a party. Pascal is standing in front of a big serving dish. Everyone at the table is laughing and talking.

"Attenzione!" I hear Pascal call out. *"Marco, la luce!* Ladies and gentlemen, I present to you!"

The lights go out, and then he takes a match and he lights the serving dish and the food goes on fire. Everybody at the table claps and hollers. They call this the Cherries Jubilee dessert in America. It is a *dolce* with cherries and brandy on the top. I think maybe to ask Primo if we can serve this dessert because people seem to like it very much, but I know what he will say.

Pascal is a very short man but he have a big voice that sounds rough when he talks, like he have a piece of metal stuck inside his throat. He always wears the best new suits, very stylish, and he looks younger than he is really because he have a full head of hair even if it is a silver color. He sees me across the room and I wave at him.

Pascal comes to America from Corsica. This is a very beautiful island in the Mediterranean Sea but it is not Italian, it is a French island. The people speak French there and another language that is a kind of Italian. Now he speaks only English, but he sounds like he is some French and some Italian and something else that you can't really figure out. I never hear an accent like his before anywhere.

"Hey, hey, fucking guy!" Pascal yells and he grabs me around the head and crushes me in a big hug and kisses me on the cheek. When Pascal says hello to you it is like you are being attacked.

"Did you see me over there?" he says. "I should be in the circus, right?" He laughs very loud at his joke. He always laughs at his own jokes. "Hey, you got everything you need? Charlie, you take care of my friend?"

"Of course," Charlie says and I say, "I am all set."

Pascal pulls me close to him. "I love this guy, he is like my brother!" he says, and he looks right into my eyes. Pascal has very blue eyes, the color of the Mediterranean, but they are not warm like that water. They can be very cold.

"You are the best, the best guy!" he says and starts to walk around me like I am a statue in the park. "And good-looking, too, huh? That's a beautiful suit. Have I seen that before?"

"Well, Pascal . . ." I say, but before I can finish a waiter comes up to the bar to get some drinks and Pascal grabs him and tells him like a sergeant tell a soldier, "Cesare, give table number six a bottle of whatever they're having on the house. But don't open it. I'll be over in one minute."

Then he turns to me and says, "So, fucking guy, you close early. What happened? You run out of food? Ha, ha, ha!"

He laughs even more loud this time, and Charlie laughs too. I laugh at his joke even though I don't see what is so funny here.

"No, no, I make a joke," Pascal says.

Big Night

"Listen, Pascal, I can talk to you one minute?" I say.

"Sure, go ahead."

"No, I mean . . ." and I point around the corner.

"Oh, in the back!" he says. "Sure, in my office, come on."

We walk through the restaurant to go to his office. Pascal stops at table number six and he opens the bottle of wine for two couples that are eating there. They all applaud him and we go on, but he stops at almost every table and everyone says hello to him. He makes jokes and laughs like hell and everyone loves this. I think this is how it should be to run a restaurant. People come and they eat your food and they have a good time and they say hello to you. You make them feel like they are having dinner in your home.

Pascal's office is big and very nice. The walls are made out of wood and he have a nice dark red leather couch I sit in. He have a big wood desk, and on the walls he have many photographs in frames of the people who have come to eat in his restaurant. Some are movie stars, some radio people, musicians, politicians. It seems to me like Pascal knows everybody in the world.

Pascal knows our business is no good. He can see with his own eyes that we don't have the kind of customers he does. But he always wants to know how we are doing and how Primo is. I don't think he is worried that we will take away business from him. He knows Primo is a chef who makes a different kind of food from the kind he serves and our place is so much smaller, not like his.

So I ask him if he can lend to me some money so I can make my payment of the mortgage. He thinks for a minute about this. But instead of saying yes or no instead he says he has another idea. He wants to know why I don't just close the business up and come and work for him at his place.

"But I am not just me," I say, "I am me and my brother, so . . ." And I shrug at him.

"So you guys cannot even think about coming to work for me," he says. "With me, I should say, with me."

"Believe me, I think about it," I say.

Pascal nods. "Yes, I see you thinking," he says.

"No, no, I am flattered," I say. I know Pascal wants us but I say nothing to Primo about this because I know what he will say. Primo does not like Pascal at all and would never want to work for him. He calls Pascal an animal but I think he is too much hard on Pascal.

"My brother," I say, "he has ideas of the way things should be."

"Ideas is ideas," Pascal says.

"Yes, you know I have to convince him to come here, to have our own place," I say. "And you know, in Italy, you work hard and there is nothing. But here, you work hard and you can go up, up, up, up, up."

"Hey baby, that is why we are all come here," Pascal says. "Land of fucking opportunity, right? But, you know, you come here, you can't have the figs the first year you plant the goddamn tree, no matter who you are. You know what I am saying?"

"I know," I say. "Is funny, this is exactly what my brother say."

Pascal shifts in his chair behind his desk.

"Yes, but, Seco, may I say something to you that I learn, without being too big?" he says and he taps at his head with a pencil.

I nod at him. I want to hear what idea he have for me. I need something.

"A guy goes out to eat at the end of the hard day, in the office, or whatever," he says, "he don't want on his plate

something he has to look and think 'What the fuck is this?',
am I right? No, he want to say, 'Oh, this is a steak, I like
steak. Mmmmm. I am happy.' You know what I mean? Now
don't get me wrong, your brother is a good goddamn chef.
Maybe the best I have ever seen."

"He is the best," I say.

"Yes, but, this is what I have to say to you," Pascal says
and he leans in to me across his desk. "Give to people what
they want. Then, later, you can give to them what *you* want."

"Pascal, believe me, I know," I say. But I shake my head
at him. I know Primo can never do this. He thinks different
from Pascal. He thinks the opposite idea. He thinks you
must give people time to learn something new. But what am
I supposed to do, sit around and wait while the bank comes
and takes away the Paradise from us?

"Fucking guy," Pascal says, "if you and your brother
come and work with me, you know you wouldn't have nothing to worry about, right?"

I nod yes but I throw up my hands to him. I know he
would take care of us, but what can I do? If we go to work
with him, I think that we can maybe help Pascal learn how
to cook better, to have more what they call "class" in this
country. More *eleganza.* But we come here to do this on our
own and I want to make it work on our own.

Pascal shakes his head at me. "But Seco, I think the kind
of money you ask me for, I can't give to you."

"That's okay," I say. "I understand. And I'm sorry if I—"

Pascal waves his hand at me. But I feel very upset now,
like I can cry. I do not know what I will do about the money,
about the bank, about Primo, or Phyllis, about everything. I
sit back in the couch and put my hands on top of my head.

"You know, everything have just become too much," I
say to Pascal.

Pascal looks at me like I am crazy. "Hey, fucking guy,

what is this?" he says. "What do you mean, too much?" All of a sudden he pounds on his desk with his fist and he jumps up from his chair like his pants are on fire and he comes around the desk to me.

"There is never too much!" he yells at me and he points up to the ceiling. *"There is only not enough! Bite your teeth into the ass of life and drag it to you!"*

Then he drops down on the couch right next to me all out of breath like he just finished swimming a mile in the ocean. He sits down too close to me so I try to move over but there is no room left on the couch for me to go anywhere.

"Well, that is why I come here to you," I say to him. Right now I need money, that's it.

"No, no, you don't need money," he says like he knows what I am thinking about. "What I am saying has nothing to do with money."

Then he leans right over me and he points to a framed photograph on the wall behind my head. "Who's that?"

I lean back and look in the picture. It is a picture of Humphrey Bogart, the movie star. He is in a tuxedo and a raincoat and it looks like it is a picture from a movie. He looks very handsome.

"Humphrey Bogart," I say.

"That's right, Humphrey Bogart, listen, I tell you a story," Pascal says. "Two years ago, he was in town. I send champagne, the best, to him at his hotel. *Complimenti di Pascal.* That's it, on my card, like that. By hand, I write. Two days later, I get that picture, there, signed to me. Now, six months go by and look, look in that picture there."

He points to another picture on the other wall. "Who do you see? Who is having dinner here in this restaurant? Tell me."

I get up from the couch and go to look at the picture. This one is taken in Pascal's and Pascal is standing next to

Humphrey Bogart and two beautiful girls. They all look very happy.

"It's Humphrey Bogart," I say.

"Humphrey Bogart," Pascal says. "You see what I mean?"

Then Pascal jumps up again and comes toward me and makes a big sound like he is a wild animal and he tries to bite me in the ass. I jump away and I almost knock down the lamp on the filing cabinet and Pascal laughs very loud. I laugh too although I think he must be a crazy man and before I can do anything else, Pascal takes me by my arm and shows me another picture on the wall. In this picture Pascal is standing next to another man. This man is chubby with curly black hair and big eyes and lips and he holds a trumpet in his hand.

"Look in this picture here," he says. "That is me with Louis Prima. You know him, right?" Pascal sings, *"Buona sera, signorina, buona sera."*

Louis Prima. I know who this guy is. I hear his music many times on the radio. He plays the trumpet and he sings jazzy songs. He sings old Italian songs that he makes all jazzed up, like "Oh Marie."

"Sure, Louis Prima, big jazz guy," I say. "I love Louis Prima."

"Friend of mine," Pascal says. I think Pascal likes to impress me with these people he knows.

"Great," I say.

"He is in town next week," he says. "You can cook for him?"

I can't believe what he is saying to me. "You want me to cook for Louis Prima?" I say.

"That's right, Louis Prima," he says. "You know, for his band, on their night off, like that. Then, maybe, word gets around, things pick up, and *la vita è dolce per tutti.*"

"Well, that sounds, yes," I say. This big jazz guy coming to the Paradise. This could be what we need to do. This will be good for the business. Then I think about Primo. I don't know if he will like this idea.

"I just have to talk to my brother," I say. But Pascal looks at me and shakes his head. "But I think I can do," I say. "Yes, I do."

"I make a call, I set it up for you," Pascal says. "Okay?"

"Okay," I say.

"C'mon, let's go check the front," he says.

When we walk down the hallway to the dining room I am already thinking about what we can serve to Louis Prima. And I think we can make a party of this and we can get the word around that we have stars at our restaurant, too. I think Gabriella knows somebody at a newspaper and I can ask her to get him to come and write a story about Louis Prima at the Paradise. People will come then because they will think we have famous people in our place all the time and think maybe they can see somebody big like Marilyn Monroe or John Wayne.

We go outside Pascal's restaurant. The night is nice with a little breeze coming in from the ocean. People are still coming in and out to eat at his place and Pascal greets them with *"Buona sera"* and chats with them. I think he is like the mayor or something.

I look over and I see Gabriella is standing there in the front of the place too, taking a break, smoking a cigarette.

Pascal says to me, "You know Gabriella."

"Oh, yes, hello," I say to her. She gives me a nod. Pascal always introduces us to each other when I come over here and we always pretend we don't know each other really.

But it is hard for me not to look at her. She is so god-damn sexy in her black dress. It falls off of one shoulder and makes her look like she is a movie star. Who needs Marilyn

Monroe? I think sometimes Gabriella looks a little like Sophia Loren with her dark eyes and dark hair and big lips. But I would never tell her this because she would only laugh at me. She laughs at me a lot.

"Pascal, listen, thank you," I say to him and I shake his hand.

"Hey, baby, c'mon, I am for you like one of those things with the lights," he says.

"What things?" I say.

"For the ships, in the storm," he says. "With the lights. What do you call them?"

"I don't know," I say. I am confused by what he is talking about.

"A lighthouse," Gabriella says from the side of her mouth.

"Yeah, a lighthouse!" Pascal says and he starts to laugh. "A goddamn lighthouse! That's what I am for you, baby, a goddamn lighthouse! If it is raining, you look for me. I show you the way home."

"Okay," I say and laugh but then Gabriella says, "Suppose he doesn't want to come home?"

"Why doesn't he want to come home?" Pascal says to her. "He's in the fucking rain."

"Some people like the rain," she says and takes another drag of her cigarette. I wonder why she is saying these things. I think she is trying to make Pascal mad and if she is she's doing a damn good job.

"It's not just rain," Pascal says, "It's a storm! He's in a goddamn storm! He should come home!"

Gabriella looks at us like she is bored. "Well," she says and she takes another drag on her cigarette. She makes me laugh, Gabriella. Sometimes I think she thinks she owns the world but she doesn't have to do too much to get it. Everything she have Pascal gives to her. All she have to do is stand around his place and look beautiful and say hello to people. She is good at this.

"Well what?" Pascal says, and now I think I should say something to stop them before they have a big fight over me right here on the street.

"No, if it's a bad storm I look for the light," I say with a laugh, "but I do like the rain."

Pascal waves his hand up to the sky. "Rain is wet and that's it!" he says like he is very angry. He turns to her and barks out, "Gabriella, go check the menus, please."

Gabriella gives Pascal a dirty look and throws her cigarette down. Then she walks back to the door and Leo opens it for her and she goes inside. Now I really want to leave but before I go I have to make sure of something first.

"Pascal, listen, can I ask you?" I say and I move close to him. "If my brother knows that you . . ."

Pascal takes my arm and he looks at me very serious. "Seco, please," he says, "that cradle will not be rocked by me. I didn't do nothing. This is all yours."

"*Grazie*," I say.

"Are you kidding?" he says. Then he pulls me more close to him and he talks low like he is a spy in the movies. "I love secrets. Secrets make friendships more strong."

He thinks this is very funny and he starts to laugh. I laugh too and then I say good night to Leo and Pascal and head back toward the Paradise. I am happy to be out of there but for the first time today I feel better. Louis Prima! At our place! This is a great thing. Now all I have to do is talk to Primo about this although I know he is going to be a pain in my neck. This should be very easy, like cooking *risotto*.

When I come upstairs to the bedroom Primo is snoring away like usual. I want to wake him up to tell him about Louis Prima and I make some noise by dropping my shoes but he doesn't move. I sit on my bed and I watch him sleep. Sometimes I think he looks like a little boy when he sleeps, he looks so peaceful and calm, not like when he is awake.

I have one week to get him to be excited about Louis Prima coming. I think I'm going to need every day.

Chapter Four

How to Make
Fresh Pasta by Hand

Pasta Fresca

Form a mound of 2 cups of all-purpose flour on a pastry board or table and make a well in the center. Break 3 eggs into the well. Beat the eggs with a fork for a minute or two and then with the other hand start to mix in the flour from the top of the mound. Add it slowly so that the mixture does not stick to the board. When the flour is almost totally absorbed, begin kneading, pressing with the heels of your palms and folding the dough for about 10 minutes or until it is well blended and smooth but still moist.

Dust the pastry board with some flour. Divide the dough into 4 balls. (Work with one ball at a time; keep the others covered.) Roll out each ball with a long thin rolling pin in a flat oval. Then turn and roll the dough several times until it is completely round. Dust it with flour and turn it over. Again roll out and turn, dust with flour, and turn over. Do this about five times. After the second or third time, it will be hard to lift and turn over the pasta by hand, so gently wrap it around the rolling pin and unroll it on the reverse side.

When the pasta is rolled out as thin as you can get it, roll on the edges to make sure the sheet is the same thickness all the way around. Try to work as quickly as you can so the dough doesn't dry out and crack. Then cut into your favorite shape by hand (or use a pasta machine). Makes enough pasta to serve 4 people.

Primo

My brother is very happy Louis Prima come to the restaurant tonight. But me, I no am so happy. I know what he think to do by have some big jazz guy come to the Paradise and have dinner. He think if we have someone famous come then everyone will come.

Sure, big deal. But what about the food I make? This is why people should come here. We are not a music show, we are a *trattoria*. I no understand why he think this way. Is like when he keep on say to me, make a meatball, make a meatball. He say in America everyone like the spaghetti and meatball. This is what people eat, he say, what they think to be Italian. We should give them what it is they like to eat.

So the other night I try to cook some meatball when it rain outside and we have no customer. My Uncle Paolo tell me any fool can make a meatball. But Seco keep talking to me about it, so I think okay, I make some meatball.

Cristiano sit with me on the butcher block when I cook the meatball and he watch. He is a good boy and he try very hard. He watch all the time and I think he know what is go on here more than he say to anybody. But he is too skinny and I try to give him more food to eat. I want to teach him about cooking like Uncle Paolo teach me. But Cristiano is not ready yet. He need more time to learn.

When I am make the meatball he tell me about a dream he have. In his dream is raining outside and man on a horse ride up to Cristiano and he say to him, "Cristiano, why don't you come in from the rain?" And the man take him in from the rain on the horse.

"Where does he take you?" I ask him.

"To my home," he say.

"To Puerto Rico?"

"I don't know where he take me," Cristiano say, "but I know I am home."

When he say something like this, sometime I think Cristiano is like the angel from God who come down to the Earth but nobody know this. He is a secret angel. He will be very quiet and then he will say something that I think is very smart and that no one else ever say.

"That's a good dream," I say to him. "Here, taste." I give him a meatball to taste and he eat it and he say it is good.

I hold one of these up to him and I tell him, "These are meatball. I only make this because my brother say we need something for these people in America think to be Italian. Like that animal make across the street. I don't mind a meatball, really, but please, can't we move on? You know what I say?"

Cristiano look at me and nod but I don't think he know what I say. Then I take a taste of the meatball.

"Uuuh!" I say and spit it out. "This is no good! How can you like this?"

I start to dump the pan of meatball into the garbage. Cristiano try to stop me.

"No, no! I eat!" he say.

"No! Nobody will eat!" I say. "You see what happen to me now? Do you see? See when you try to do something that is not even what it is you want to do? Do you see?"

Now I am mad at my brother for wanting me to cook this. I take the meatball one by one and I throw them in the garbage. Cristiano keep on try to stop me but I don't want to see these on my stove anymore.

"It doesn't matter," I say. "I can't cook. I know nothing

about cooking. Because I am not a cook. I am nothing. I am, maybe, someone who wants to be a cook! And so, what I should do, is I should decide to be something else, and then I no will have to live in the life of torture I am live in!"

I throw the pot into the garbage. Cristiano look at me like I am a crazy man and I walk away from him to the outside. If I am crazy, it is because my brother make me this way. Meatball, please, *Dio mio.*

All this week Seco talk about Louis Prima. Louis Prima, Louis Prima, this is all I hear. He want to plan the menu for when Louis Prima come. I say sure. We make a menu and then he change his mind. What if Louis Prima no like this dish? What if Louis no like that? He make me so tired about Louis Prima. Is like the Queen of England is come here.

I worry sometime about my brother because he think when Louis Prima come everything will now be better. I no see how it can make everything be better. He is just one guy. But I say nothing to Seco. Sometimes it is better to just say nothing.

Now today is the day we must get ready for Louis Prima. Seco is drive the car because we are come back from the fish market. We get up very early this morning with the sun to go there. This is how you get a good fish, you go early, otherwise everything is gone that is good.

Seco always say that these fish guys try to cheat you. They try to sell you fish that is bad or have worm. But our uncle teach us how to buy a good fish. When you look at the fish, the fish must feel very firm when you touch. If the flesh bounce back when you touch and you leave no the mark of your finger there, then it is fresh. He also tell me to look in the eye too. The eye should be bright like the sun and clear like the water and be bulge out like a fat stomach. We get a big salmon and we have it on the ice in our backseat because it can't fit in the trunk, that's how big this fish is.

I never see Seco so excite about something before except
when we first come here to America. He is all excite about
tonight and he is talk very fast. He say to me, "That son of a
bitch fish man. See how he change his song? 'Louis Prima,
at our place, tonight.' That's all I have to say and boom—we
get the best fish. What time is it? Fuck, we gotta hurry.
Later, remind me to call the pastry chef. Do I have enough
tomato? Do we have enough tomato?"

"Yes," I say, but I no care too much one way or the other
way.

He look over at me. "What's the matter with you? Are
you sick?"

"No, I'm fine," I tell him. "You talk to Phyllis?"

"Why?"

"I just am asking."

"Yeah, the other day," he say.

"How is she?"

"Who are you, Elliot Ness?" he say. "She's doing great.
Never better."

I know he no talk to her because I talk to Phyllis myself.
I can always tell when things are no good with him and Phyllis because he is in a bad mood all the time and he say his
stomach bother him and he yell at Cristiano a lot. So I call
her on the telephone the other day and she tell me they have
a fight. She say all he think about is the restaurant. I say I
know this but I know he want to see her. I tell her about
Louis Prima coming. Now he try to lie to me about her but
I play the game with him.

"Good," I say to Secondo. "I like Phyllis."

"So do I," he say. "Okay, now, the wine. What do you
think?"

I shrug my shoulder at him and look out the window. I
no care really what wine he want. This is for me no big deal

if Louis Prima come or no. I know he want me to be excite about this party but like I say I think this is a stupid idea.

"I have a friend, just listen, can get us a nice *barolo,*" he say. "Cheap."

"If you like," I say.

"Primo, please," he say. "*Madonna miseria,* why still do you continue to resist? Why? I need your help here. This is not just some guy! This is Louis Prima. He's famous."

"Famous," I say. "Is he good?"

"He's great," Seco say.

I no care if he is Giuseppe Verdi and he bring Enrico Caruso with him.

"People should come just for the food," I tell Seco.

"I know that."

"They should come just for the food," I say again. That's it.

"I know that," Seco say and then he turn his head to look at me very serious. "But they don't."

We say nothing after this, we just drive. It no is my fault if these people here don't like the food we make. If they don't like and we can't wait for them to like, then we should just go back home to Italia. Why stay here when no one want what you do?

Secondo stop the car in front of the flower shop where I go to buy the flowers for our restaurant. He say he have to go to the bank. We get out of the car and Seco stop when he see in front of us one of those big, black American cars. Is very shiny and new.

"Oh, boy, Cadillac, the newest," Secondo say. He look at this car like he is in love. I know he want to have this car instead of the rusty old one he have. I don't care, really, because I never learn how to drive the car. Where I come from you just walk everywhere you need to go. To the church, to the market, everything is near and you can see everyone if you just walk, you no have to drive. Here in America everybody drive around all over the place like crazy people.

Seco walk around this car and he look in the window. "Beautiful, huh?" he say. "Cadillac."

"Big," I say to him and I go to the door of the flower shop, but he stop me at the door.

"Primo, tell her to make them something, you know, for tonight," he call to me. "And Primo, ask her if she want to come tonight."

I no pay attention to him and then I go inside the flower shop. The little bell rings on the door and I can smell all the flower as soon as I walk in. There are so many different color of flower in Ann's store, like the different color of the *antipasti* when you put them all together on the table.

Ann own this flower shop because her husband open it before he die. She tell me another time when I am here her husband die in the World War II. He was a flier in the airplane and he got shot down in the Pacific. She only was a young girl when she marry him right before he go away to the war, twenty, twenty-one years old. She no marry anyone else since then.

Ann is a tall woman and pretty, with very long legs and arms, no like a movie star, but a quiet pretty. She no look like any of the girls from our town in Italy. In Italy the girls are dark and have dark hair and eyes. Ann look more American, she have brown hair and her eyes are very big. She open them up very wide when she talk.

When I come in she is talk on the telephone to someone. "This is ridiculous," I hear her say in the phone, "I had five orders to deliver." I wave at her and she wave back.

She listen in the phone and then she say, "Well, I'm

afraid I'm going to be unable to recommend you to anyone in the future. No, that's all I have to say to you. Good-bye." And she hang up.

"Trouble today?" I say.

Ann smile at me. I like very much the way she smile.

"I won't even . . . some people," she say and look down at her hands. "I'm sorry, I'm afraid I don't have your irises today. The delivery didn't come."

"Somebody no do their job?" I say.

"Yes, somebody didn't think it was very important," she say. Her big eyes, they are like the green of the arugula.

"Oh, that is even more worse," I say.

"C'mon, we'll find something else," she say, and she go over to the big flower case. I am nervous in here because now I think to maybe ask her to come to the restaurant, tonight to the party, but I don't know how I can.

I go over to the case and I say to her, "I think for tonight, my brother, he want something, you know—" but I stop because I forget what word I want to say.

"Special?" she say.

"Special, yes," I say. She is very good with me when I can't speak my English. She have the patience and she help me with the word.

"Some big jazz guy is coming," I say. "Louis Prima."

"Oh, I love Louis Prima," Ann say.

"Oh you know him? He is good?"

"Very good," she say. "Boisterous."

I do not know what this word mean and Ann can see. "Um, he has lots of energy," she say.

"Oh, good, that's good," I say and I smile at her. But I think I smile at her too long, because then I see in her face I am stare at her. So I start to look at all the flowers in the case.

"Yes, I don't know, something special," I say. I am *molto nervoso* standing so next to her. She smell so good, she smell like the flowers.

"These are nice," she say, pointing to some gladiolas.

I am so nervous with her I go right into the inside of the case and I look at the flowers. I no even know what I am do in there or what I am see in there because I smell Ann and I smell all the flowers and I want to ask her to come to the party but I am afraid to ask. I walk two step in the inside of the case and I just pull out one white flower and I step back down and out of the case and I hand Ann the flower. I can see she try to no laugh at what I do.

"Listen, I could get something together for you and bring it over this afternoon," she say and she smile at me again.

"Okay," I say, "okay." I close the big door on the flower case. I think I should better go now before I look more stupid, but I no want to go yet. I start to walk to the door. I think now to ask her.

I say to her, "So I guess you will close early tonight."

"Why?"

"Because I thought of the no delivery," I say.

"Oh, yes, I guess I'll have to," Ann say. "But it doesn't matter. I've just started a new book, so I guess I'll just go home and get in the tub."

I know what I want to say then but all I say is "Oh, good." I can't even talk anymore. Inside my head, I am ask her to come to the party, but my feet and my legs instead are walk me to the door, and when I get there all I can say is thank you to her.

"Well, thank you," she say. "And good luck tonight."

"Oh, yes, thanks," I say. I start to open the door to go out and then I turn back and I say to her, "What is the story?"

She turn around and she look at me like I am a crazy man. "I'm sorry?" she say.

"In the book," I say. "The story in the book."

"Oh," she say, "the pioneers."

"Oh, the wild west, Buffalo Bill," I say and I make like with my hands like I am shooting off some gun. I hear about this on the radio, the cowboy and the alone ranger.

Ann laughs. "Well, sort of," she say. "Families on the trail."

"Oh, yes, tough times," I say like I know what I am saying.

"Well, times are always tough for somebody," she say.

I laugh at this, and I keep laughing a lot because I am so nervous and she is so beautiful. She look at me and give me a smile. Then I think I better go now.

"Well, I'm taking a long time here, so, thank you, and I hope you like the book," I say, "and I hope that the pioneers are, you know, okay."

She look at me like she is confuse and then I know Ann want me to ask her to come to the party but is too hard for me to do so I open the door and I get out of there.

I go back to the car and I get in. I am very hot now and I sweat. I close my eyes and wait for my brother to come back and take me home. It smell all like fish in the car and I just want to get back to the Paradise to start to cook.

When Seco come back to the car, he don't ask me if I ask Ann to come to the party. He is think about something. He don't look so happy and I think it is because of the bank. He never look happy when he come from the bank. We say nothing to each other when we drive back to the restaurant. We both are just think.

When we get home, we see Alberto and Ida outside the barber shop. Ida is sweep the sidewalk and Alberto is read his paper. They wave hello to us.

Big Night

We get the fish from the car and Ida call out, "Hey boys, you go fishing?" and Seco call to her, "It's beautiful, huh?" and he hold up the fish for her to see. Then we hear a horn honk very loud and we see Pascal and Gabriella come by in his big car. I think probably they are stay out all night because they still are wear dress-up clothes.

Pascal slow down his car when he see us with the fish and he yell, "Hey, boys, I see you tonight! Hey, Michelangelo, *come stai?*" I hear him laugh a big laugh and Gabriella wave at us. When Pascal say Michelangelo he mean me. He think this to be funny that he call me Michelangelo. Ha, ha.

"You invite him?" I ask Seco.

"I invite everybody," he say. This make me mad. I have to make the food for this dinner I no even want to cook and now I have to cook for this *cane* across the street. Seco should tell me he ask Pascal to come.

When we go inside the kitchen Cristiano is there already and he chop up carrot for the dinner tonight. He always chop too fast, Cristiano, so I tell him to go slow, slow.

"Good morning, good morning, nice fish," he say when he see us. "There is no hot water."

"What?" Secondo say.

"Nothing comes out."

I go to the sink and I turn on the faucet for the hot. There is nothing come out. These pipe make us all crazy.

"FUCK!!" Secondo say. "Maybe I should just ask the goddamn plumber to move in with us!"

He drop down the fish on the table and he start to go to the dining room.

"Where do you go?" I say.

"To Hollywood!" he say. "I'm going to call the fucking plumber, where do you think!?" He say to Cristiano, "Did Chubby come yet?"

"Not yet," Cristiano say.

"Fat fuck, he's late," Seco say and he go out to the dining room. Cristiano look at me. I shrug my shoulder. I don't know why brother get so upset about these pipe. They break all the time, that is because they are old and we need new pipe. The plumber can fix. He worry too much, Secondo. I think he is mad about the bank not about the pipe and now he is start to worry about tonight and Louis Prima. He always worry.

I put the fish away in the icebox and then we hear Chubby's truck come in the backyard. Every day he is come with his truck and the fruit and vegetable delivery. He is call Chubby because he is a fat man. He wear big glasses. Chubby have a good heart but I think sometime he try to cheat us like the fish man.

I go outside to see Chubby and say hello to him. He always joke with me, Chubby. I think he do this so I don't pay too much attention to his vegetable because sometime they are no so good. But Seco say he have the best price around, so we do our business with him.

Chubby start to show me what he have today. Some red pepper, very nice. Some good zucchini, no too big. Is better when the zucchini are small, they taste more sweet. Then he show me some basil. They look mostly black. I sniff them and they no smell too bad, but they are no good, and really no good for tonight.

"Small," I say to Chubby.

"They're small, but they're fine," he say. Then Seco come out of the restaurant and he say hi to Chubby and then he take the basil from me and smell it.

"Are they fresh?" he ask Chubby.

"Fresh today," say Chubby. I know he lie to us. Anyone can see this basil is not fresh today.

"C'mon, looks dead, like a wig," I say to him.

"I'm sorry, Primo, that's it," he say. "That's all the basil I got today."

"Well, we need them," Seco say and he look at me. He want me to say the basil is okay. The basil is not okay. This basil is lousy basil.

"Well, it's your party," I say to Seco. I start to look at other vegetable. I hear my brother sigh at me like he is mad.

"Primo, *vieni qui*," he say. "Chubb, do you mind, I want to talk to my brother one minute."

"Sure," Chubby say.

Then Secondo take my arm and he take me over to the back door of the restaurant so Chubby can't hear what he say. He look at me very hard.

"Primo, this dinner tonight is happening," he say.

"Certo," I say. Right. But this no mean I have to like it.

"Do you know why?" he ask me.

I know why. Seco want to be a big shot. He want everyone to know he know all the famous people. He want to change everything in our place to be American. But I no say this. I just shrug at him.

"Because it has to happen," he say. "We need to do this. Do you understand me?"

I shake my head no at him. I no need to do nothing. I am fine.

"Money," he say.

I no understand what he mean. Seco always take care of the money. I know we don't have many customer lately but I never think it is so serious. I think it is just Seco get nervous like he do about everything. So this is why he is so mad when he come from the bank.

"But I thought . . ."

"No," say Seco, "this is it."

"But why you no tell me?" I ask.

"And what were you gonna do?" he say.

He no have to say this to me. I never take care of the money because he always take care of it. I take care of other thing. I know when the basil is good and when it is no so good. I know how many chicken to buy for the day so we no buy too many or too enough.

"I'm sorry," he say. He look away for a minute at Chubby and the vegetable and then he turn back to me. I can tell from how he look he is be very serious now.

"After tonight I don't know how much longer we can do what we came here to do," he say. "The way we want to do it. Do you understand me?"

I don't know what to say, I can't believe he say this. We are here only two year. I know it is not so easy to be in this country and I miss my family very much but Seco and me work so hard already to come here, to make a good place here. And now he say that everything is come to one night, this night.

"Okay? Is that . . . ?" Seco say.

I nod yes to him.

"Okay," he say. "Good."

Seco go back to Chubby and say, "Sorry, Chubb."

"What are you guys, choosin' the new pope?" I hear Chubby say and laugh. "So what we decide?"

"We'll take it," Seco say. "What else you got?"

"What's goin' on?" Chubby ask Seco and Seco tell him about Louis Prima is come to the restaurant and he ask Chubby if he want to come tonight. I no hear what Chubby say because I am think about tonight. I understand now why Seco is so excite and nervous for Louis Prima to be at our place. If we are in trouble with money then I guess we must make this meal for Louis Prima the best we know to make.

❊   ❊   ❊

I go inside to the bar to get a glass of *acqua minerale* and there is Phyllis in the phone booth. I guess she and Seco are better now, because she say she is come here to help us with the party. She talk to Seco before he come out to see Chubby. I am glad she come, because now we have so much work to do to make a good meal. She say she call the plumber to come back and take care of the pipe. I kiss her on the cheek and she kiss me back. She is a nice girl, Phyllis.

"So everything is working out okay?" I ask her.

"So far," she say. "Thanks for calling me."

"Sure, sure," I say to her. "I know he want you to be here, but sometime he is too, you know, crazy to call you himself."

She nod at me and smile. She know about Secondo. I drink my water. I am think about the basil and the no money and tonight. I see now this night is a big deal for us, not just a party Seco want to have to look good. We must make something—what is the word Ann say?—something special for tonight.

Phyllis look at me and say, "What's wrong?"

I just shrug at her and I hold out my hand to her and she take it. "C'mon," I say and I take her into the kitchen. Seco come back inside too with a bag of onion from Chubby and he start to open.

"I called the plumber," Phyllis say to him. "He said he'll be over lickety-split."

Seco just grunt at her and I think he is mad at me because he have to talk to me in front of Chubby and he is nervous about tonight. I go the storeroom and I get my white chef jacket and start to put it on. Phyllis can see something is no good with me and Seco and she say very happy, "So, where do we start?"

I know what I want to make now to be special for Louis Prima, so I say, "Yes Phyllis, may I ask you to get me that white tub from over there, please? And Cristiano, my friend, that other one."

Secondo know what I think to do and he yell at me, "No!"

Phyllis give me the white basin from under the table and Cristiano get the other one from up on the shelf where we keep the dish. "And now we must clean them," I say to them. It is a long time since I use these tubs and I know they have dust.

Secondo say, "Primo, no! *Timpano?* Are you crazy? There is not the time!"

"Seco, you start the rabbit," I say and I throw a pot to him.

Phyllis say, "What's *timpano?*"

Secondo is mad again. "Primo, no, I have to be serious here!"

I say to him, "Seco, you tell me this is a big night."

"What is this you're making, exactly?" Phyllis want to know. Seco tell her to go and call the plumber to fix the pipe but Phyllis say she already call him. Seco get very upset and start to hit the pot on his head and yell at poor Cristiano, but I ignore him and tell Phyllis about the *timpano*.

The *timpano* is a kind of pasta dish that you cook inside a crust, a pastry crust. It is a very old recipe that come from my mother and her mother and her mother. It is call *timpano* because you put all the ingredients in the tub that is shape like a drum, like a timpani drum they have in the orchestra. Then you bake in the oven for a long time.

"And inside," I tell Phyllis, "are all the most important things in the world!"

Phyllis think this sound good and she want to help make this *timpano*. She tell Seco he is act like a baby and to let me do what I want. Seco grumble about how we have too much else to do today besides make the *timpano*. I just pay no attention to him and we start to clean the tub. Then he start to talk about the *timpano* and how much he like and then I think he is glad to make this because he know that Louis Prima will like. Everyone like a *timpano*.

So all this morning we work very hard. First we make some fresh *garganelli* pasta for the soup. I like to make our pasta by hand because I like better than the pasta that come in the box. I want to make too a big table of the *antipasti* like my uncle have at his *trattoria*. People like to eat this before we serve the meal because they can have many choice, many different kind of food. We make some *focaccia* bread with rosemary, we grill some red and yellow pepper, and we start to make the *crostini* with the olive oil and goat cheese.

Then I roll out the pastry crust for the *timpano*, and Phyllis and Seco help to put the *timpano* together in the tub. This take some time. You have to put in some *ziti* pasta, eggs that are hard boil, some meat and salami, and *sugo marinara*. Then we let it rest before we bake later.

Then the plumber come and Seco almost have a fistfight with him because he call the plumber a thief. The plumber get very mad too and he say he no will fix the pipe at all if Seco call him a thief. Thanks to God Phyllis is there and she make everybody calm down and then we get back our hot water. But Seco is still very mad and he say he think this plumber should go to jail because he think he is like a gangster.

After a few hour we all get hungry and we need to rest, so I make some *spaghetti con aglio e olio* for lunch. We all eat together, Cristiano too, in the dining room. Seco talk a lot about Louis Prima and he tell us about how he is a big star, he play in a place call Las Vegas and make record albums and movies too. Phyllis say he is marry to a girl singer called Keely who is a very good singer, too.

Phyllis like to sing, too. I hear her sing all the time to herself when she work. She start to hum a song and she get up and go to Cristiano. "Cristiano, come dance with me," she say.

"No, no, no, no, no," Cristiano say. I see he is embarrass. But she pull him up from his seat anyway and they start to dance in the middle of the dining room while she hum some jazz music. Cristiano look like a skinny chicken when he dance. He look so funny. I see he is shy around Phyllis.

Seco is smoke a cigarette and we sit and watch them dance. Seco call out to Cristiano, "Hey, hey, you steal my girl?"

"*No, no me gusta las mujeres porque muchas problemas,*" Cristiano say and he pull away from Phyllis.

"I am not a *problemas,*" Phyllis say but Cristiano come back to the table and shake his head and he sit back down. Phyllis turn to Secondo and say, "C'mon, honey, it's your turn."

"No, please, I have too much to do," Seco say.

"C'mon, just for a sec," she say and wave him over to her. He get up and they dance. They look very nice together when they dance. Cristiano watch them and he look at me and smile. I see Seco looking around at all the painting we hang on the wall when he dance.

"Maybe, I think we should take down some of these for tonight," he say. "Don't you think it's too a mess?"

"Why would you do that?" Phyllis say. "They're from your friends."

Cristiano go to answer the phone when it ring and it is for Seco. He stop his dance with Phyllis and he go the phone booth and say hello and then he listen and he laugh like he is nervous about something. "Oh, no, I don't think I can right now," he say in the phone. "Oh, no. What? Okay, I be right over."

He hang up and he call to me, "Primo, I have to go see a guy about the booze. I'll be back in one hour."

"What should I do?" Phyllis ask him.

"Don't worry, Primo will show you," Seco say and he kiss her and go out the door.

Phyllis watch after him. She come back to the table and look at me and shrug. I smile at her. I think she was happy to dance with Seco and now he is gone very fast. I want to tell her that he leave all the time, Seco. He can't sit still, my brother. I don't know where he have to go all the time. But I say nothing except, "Cristiano, help me clean this up," and we all start to clean up the table.

Chapter Five

Spaghetti with Garlic and Oil

Spaghetti con Aglio e Olio

Cook 1 pound of spaghetti in salted boiling water until *al dente*, tender but firm to the bite, and drain in a colander. In the meantime, in a skillet that is big enough to hold the pasta later, combine ½ cup of extra-virgin olive oil, 4–6 gloves of garlic that have been chopped in small pieces, and a pinch of salt. Cook over medium heat until the garlic just turns golden. Watch as it cooks and be careful not to burn the garlic as this will ruin everything. (Some people like hot pepper with this dish. If you do, add ½ teaspoon crushed red pepper flakes to the oil as well.)

Add the drained spaghetti to the skillet and toss with the sauce until it is thoroughly coated. Cover the skillet and take off the heat for a minute so that the pasta will absorb the sauce. Add some chopped flat-leaf parsley if you like, and a few twists of freshly ground black pepper. Toss again and transfer to pasta bowls. Serve immediately. You should not serve cheese with this pasta. Makes 4 servings.

Secondo

Now we really have no money.

When I left Primo at the flower lady's shop, I went to the bank. I looked for Phyllis behind the bars but she was not there and I asked the teller who helped me where she was. The teller told me that Phyllis was not come in to work today. I thought if she is sick or something and I felt bad because I didn't call her since the night we went to the movies. I hope she is okay.

I took out nearly all the money we have in the bank to make this party. We have only sixty-two dollars left. I know I am crazy to spend this money on one party but I have no choice. We have to make the best party we can for Louis Prima and that means spending money. Everyone who comes to this party has to know how good we are.

I went back to the car and right away I could see Primo did not ask Ann to come tonight. His face looked all white, like he just saw a ghost or something, so I left him alone. I was thinking about the money anyway and I didn't want to say anything to him about it. So we just rode home without saying anything to each other.

After we come back from the fish market and after we put away the fish and Cristiano told us about the hot water I went to the dining room to call that thief the plumber. When I go in, I heard the record player playing a Louis Prima song. "Oh, Marie, Oh, Marie, in your arms I'm longing to be." This is an old Italian folk song that he turn into a jazz song. I don't know who made the record go on and when I went to turn it off I felt hands on my eyes and I heard Phyllis's voice say, "It's Louis Prima!" I screamed and jumped around and it was Phyllis. I scared her too because I screamed so loud.

"Phyllis!" I yelled. "You scare me! What are you do here?"

"I told my boss my mother was ill!" she said, all out of breath and laughing. "He doesn't know my mother is never ill! He doesn't even know my mother!"

"Good, good," I said. She looked very beautiful, but maybe a little tired like she was worried about something.

"So, how are you?" she asked.

"I'm fine," I said. "How are you?"

"Fine, I'm fine."

I was embarrassed because I did not call her since the other night when we had a fight. But I didn't want to call her. I wanted to take some time not to think about her and only think about the business. I'm sorry, but that's what I had to do.

"I didn't call you," I said.

"I know," Phyllis said. "I didn't call you either."

"That's true."

"I figured with tonight and everything you'd need some help," she said, and she smiled at me. "So, I'm here." The light from the morning was coming from the window and going in her hair.

"I am glad you're here," I said.

Then Cristiano poked his head in to say that Chubby is come. So I said I have to go see Chubby and asked her to call the goddamn plumber again because the water is out again. Then I kissed her but we were both nervous about seeing each other again so we almost missed each other when we kissed. But I am glad she come to help us.

She help me and Primo all morning. She is a big help

and it is good she come over because I think she keep us from fighting over everything. But then I get the phone call after we eat lunch. I have to hide who it is from her and say I am going to see a guy about the booze. That is the truth, I am going to see a guy about the booze, but later. First I have to stop and get his address and I don't want her to know who it is I am getting the address from.

I get in my car and start to drive down the street past Pascal's restaurant. Just as I go by I can't believe what I see. The chef from Pascal's, I don't know his name because they change all the time, is running down the alley and his apron is all on fire! He is screaming and running and he try to take off the apron and he finally throws it down on the ground and runs away down the street. Then Pascal comes running right behind him, and Leo, too.

Pascal screams at the chef, *"You motherfucker! Next time I light your goddamn hair on fire!"* He has his silver cigarette lighter in his hand and he shakes it at the poor chef. The fire was no accident—it was Pascal.

Then Pascal sees me driving by and all of a sudden he is Mr. Nice Guy. He waves and he call out to me, like nothing at all is going on, "Hey, fucking guy! Everything okay? I see you later!"

I can't believe this, but I wave back at him. Then I hear him say to Leo, "Where does that fucking chef live?" and they go back in the alley.

This make me very nervous to see this with Pascal. I know he is sometimes crazy but I never think he would put a man on fire. But I am the most nervous because of where I am going. I am going to Gabriella's to get her to call this guy for me so I can get a good deal on the booze. On the phone she tell me that I have to come right over if I want to get the guy's name and where he is from her. I know what she mean by this.

Big Night

She live in a very nice old apartment building in one of our town's good neighborhoods. Good cars on the street and lots of trees everywhere. Gabriella makes out okay for herself.

When I go into her place, she is in the kitchen sitting on the table talking on the phone. I kiss her and I show her my watch because I don't have much time today and I know that she will take a long time unless I tell her to hurry up. Then I go to get a drink from the sink.

"You should cut his hands off," she says into the phone. "Well, if he ever touched me, that's what I would do, cut his hands off. Well, if he's a prick, cut his prick off. Or break his hands. Or just one hand. As, you know, a warning."

This is just what I want to hear right now. First a chef on fire and now this. I don't even want to know who she's talking to. She smiles at me and waves me over to her. She is wearing only a robe over her bra and panties and she pulls me to her and starts to touch me. I feel her body and I point to my watch again to show her I am in a hurry. She starts to take off her panties while she talks.

"She did?" she says into the phone. "I thought she was dead already! Listen, I gotta go. Okay. Be good. 'Bye!"

I go to see Gabriella every once in a while. Phyllis doesn't know of course and Primo doesn't know either. I pray to God in Heaven Pascal doesn't know. I don't think he does. We are careful. Gabriella doesn't say anything, she is very good at keeping to herself. This is one of the things I like about her the best.

I don't even know really where Gabriella comes from. One day she is just with Pascal and then another day and then she is always with Pascal. She is Italian and she is from near Rome, I know that. But she never talks about how she came to this country or where she has been before Pascal. I don't think she wants anybody to know where. I know she has been around some because she is probably about forty years old and she is not married or has any children. At least not any I hear about. You never know with her.

Sometimes she says she is engaged to Pascal and she even has a ring but I think it is just a ring. I don't think Pascal would ever marry anybody. Then he would have to give half of everything he owns to them and I can't ever see Pascal doing this. This way he gets the best of everything. He gets Gabriella but she doesn't really get him. I think they both are happy with this setup.

Later I wake up in her bedroom after we sleep a little bit from making love. It is warm in her room. I look at my watch. *Madonna miseria.* I tap her on her shoulder and I say, "I have to go." I get up from the bed and start to pull on my pants.

"You're so fast today," Gabriella says, stretching out like a cat.

"I have no time," I say.

"You have time," she says and she reaches her hand out to me from the bed. I want to go back to her but I know I have to keep going if I will get everything done for the party. I know Primo is already wondering why I'm not come back yet.

"Gabriella, no, not today."

She frowns at me. She has the darkest eyes I've ever seen on a woman. "You worry like an old man," she says.

"Yeah, well, I'm not as old as some," I tell her.

"Or as rich," she says and she rolls over in the sheets and she laughs at me.

"After tonight," I say.

"After tonight, what, Secondo?" She laughs at me again and she sits back in the bed. This pisses me off for good. I know she is with Pascal because he buys her everything she have, whatever she want. This apartment, her clothes, everything. All she have to do is stand around and look beautiful for the customers at his place. Some job.

"Can you call the booze guy, please?" I say to her, very hard. I want her to know I'm not taking any shit from her today. I have too much to do today.

She sighs and picks up the phone. I start to fix my shirt and my hair in the mirror. My face looks like I am tired. Maybe I am getting like an old man.

"You know, not everybody just have everything given to them with a silver lining," I say to her. "We could serve the shit like at your old man's place. Very easy. But what we try to do take some time, you know? Work. You know what that is, right? Work?"

"Hello, Mike, I'm Gabriella," she says into the phone and then she laughs like she is a girl in school. "You can do me a favor, Mike? I have a friend who come by later—"

"No, now, I'm coming now, I'm coming now—"

"—and maybe you can help him? Yes, he needs, I don't know what he needs, he will tell you, and you give him a nice deal, huh, Mike? Oh, you are the best of them all, Mike. I tell you, Mike, whenever your wife leaves you, you call me, okay? Okay, love ya. 'Bye, Mike."

She hangs up and writes on a piece of paper near the phone.

"Who's that?" I say. I can't believe who she knows.

"Mike," she says, very cold, and she hands me the paper with the address of Mike on it.

"*Grazie,*" I say. She sits back down in the bed and she turns her body away from me. "You're coming tonight, right?" I ask her. Now I can see she is pissed off for sure at me.

"Sure," she say, "spend some time with your girlfriend."

"Gabriella, c'mon," I say. All of a sudden she has to make a big deal about Phyllis? She never talks about Phyllis very much. She knows I see Phyllis but I never say that I am very serious about Phyllis or anything like that.

She stares away from me at the wall. "Come here," I say and I try to put my arm around her and kiss her.

"*Vai, vai,*" she says and pushes me away from her. I don't want her to be pissed off at me. Not today. I want everything to be good for tonight. I want her to come and see what we do at the Paradise and have a good time. She has never been at our place for dinner and now she has a reason to come with Pascal.

"You are so beautiful," I say. I hear somebody in the movies one time say this about a woman, that she is the most beautiful when she is pissed off. That is Gabriella.

"Go," she say without looking at me. "Go get your cheap booze."

I know I can't say anything else to her that she wants to hear. I want to stay but I have to go get this booze. So I leave her.

I drive to the address Gabriella gives me and it's in the other part of town where I don't go too much. It's on the way out of town, out near where there are some factories. When I park the car and get out I am on a street with houses in not too good shape. There is junk in the street and little kids are running all around and they all look like they need to get in the bath.

The number on the address is 1451 White Street. But I see a 1449 which is a house and then next to this a big church and then next to this a 1455. But no 1451. This means that 1451 is this church, but how can this Mike the booze guy be in a church? He can't be in this church. But then I think it is Gabriella who gives me this address and who knows who she knows? I don't know where else to go so I go up the stairs of the church. The sign says Saint Peter's Church. This is a Catholic church.

I go inside the doors and it is very dark and very cool and it takes me a minute before my eyes can see inside. I touch the holy water in the little holder at the back of the church and make a fast cross. I have not been to church in a very long time. In Italy I go on the big days like Christmas and Easter but not too much else. In Italy it is like the church is in everybody's life like the air or the water so it doesn't matter really if you go to church or not. The church comes to you.

Some old women are sitting in two pews in the back and they are saying the rosary. This is what my aunt do and all the women do back home. They pray for everybody's sins and for the people who are dead. I think I should ask these ladies to say a prayer for me and maybe that will work.

I start to walk down the aisle and look up at the walls. There are big stain-glass windows on the walls and then up above near the ceiling there are small ones. From the building you can see this is a very old church. I didn't know there was a church this old and this beautiful in our town.

I look up at the altar and there is a priest standing in front and he have his back to me. He is getting the altar ready for the Mass. He has a linen for the altar and he opens it up and lays it down and smooths it out with his hands. He picks up the gold chalice for the wine and he starts to rub it with a cloth to clean it and make it shine. Then he does the same thing with the plates for the hosts. This looks like he is getting ready for a dinner, too.

I go up to the rail at the front and I look down at the paper that Gabriella give me. I don't know how this can be where she wants me to go.

"Mike?" I call out to the priest. He turns around. I see he is very young this priest. He looks like he is only a kid.

Not like Father O'Brien from the church Primo go to. Father O'Brien is an old man.

"May I help you?" the young priest says and he puts down the host plate and he comes to the rail. He have on big eyeglasses and he looks very smart.

"I am lost," I say. "Is this . . . ?"

I show him the paper. The priest reads it and smiles at me.

"It's a warehouse?" I say.

"It's through the alley," the priest says and points behind him. "Behind here. In the back."

"Thank you," I say.

"You're welcome," the priest says and he looks me over and nods at me. Then he says with a big smile, "There's a collection box for your donation in the rear of the church."

"Yes, thank you," I say and I start to walk back down the aisle. I look back at him and he is back at the altar cleaning the plates. I keep walking and go outside the church. I go right past the collection box. It is the same no matter if you are in Italy or America. It's always money with this church. What they want really is the money.

I go around the church but this Mike the booze guy is not there when I get to the address. The warehouse is closed and there is just a big truck loaded with booze parked in the front. There are two big guys on the truck and one of them tells me Mike is not there and I have to come back in a half hour and then he'll be there. I can see the booze right there on the truck but this guy won't do anything until Mike is there. This makes me mad because I have no time to wait around all day. I have to get back. But I need this booze, so while I wait I go for a walk down the street.

A little bit down I see a sign that says CADILLAC, STANDARD OF THE WORLD. In this big parking lot there are the most Cadillacs I have ever seen. White, green, black, silver, all shiny, all new. They are the most unbelievable cars I have ever seen. I walk around and look at them for a minute. There is nobody around the place so I look into this white car that have a red interior. This car is beautiful. It looks like the kind of car you have a dream about.

Then I hear a whistle, and a man's voice says, "You in the market?" But I can't see any man. Then I hear another whistle, and I think *che pazzo*, and then the man says again, "You in the market?" I look, and I see there is a man sitting inside the Cadillac next to the white one, a beautiful black one with chrome all around.

I don't understand what this man means. I don't see any market. Then he says to me, "Good-looking fella like you should have a good-looking car like this."

I laugh and I say to him, "Yes, well, there's a lot we should all have."

The man gets out of the car on the passenger side. I don't know what he was doing sitting in the car by himself. He is wearing a blue suit and I see he is the car dealer. He wants to sell me one of these cars. Good luck to him.

"I detect an accent," he says. "Where are you from?"

"I am Italian," I say.

"Just visiting or moved here for good?"

"I will never go back," I say.

"Oh, there's a history, huh?"

"In Italy," I say, "there is nothing but history."

The dealer laughs. "Funny," he says. He comes around the car and I see that his left hand is in a cast like it is broken. In his other hand he have a round candy on a stick that he keeps putting in his mouth.

"Beautiful place, though, Italy," he says.

"Yes," I say. "You been?"

"No, never," he says. "Go on, get in."

I don't want to get in, because I don't have very much

time. I look at my watch and I know that Primo is wondering where I am. But the dealer insists, and since I have never been inside this kind of car, I say okay. Just for a minute, maybe.

You can't believe how beautiful this car is on the inside. Everything is shiny on the dashboard and there are dials all over the place and there is a new radio. The front seat is so big and it makes me want to cry, it is so nice. I run my hand over it.

"That's real leather trim," the dealer says. He leans into the car from the outside. "Full air, power brakes, automatic transmission."

"This is, boy, beautiful," I say. "This is the new one? This is this year's car?"

"No, this is next year's," he say.

"Really?" I say. This is very funny to me. How can this be? "This year you buy next year's car," I say, "and then next year, next year's car comes out already, again."

"Yeah," he says and he looks at me like everybody already knows this. He have a very serious face, this guy. I think he should be more happy to sell this kind of nice car but he don't seem too happy to me.

"You got kids?" he asks me.

"No."

"I got two kids," he says. "They see their friend with a new toy? They gotta have it. And there's enough tension in my house, you know what I mean?"

"Sure, I understand," I say.

"Don't get me wrong, a Cadillac will last forever," he says. "But I'm just saying, people, in general, not you, need to have the latest thing. I'm Bob. What's your name?"

He holds out his hand and I shake it.

"Secondo."

"A pleasure," he says.

I point to the cast on his hand and ask, "What did you do to your hand?"

"I hurt it," he says.

"How?"

"I have no idea," he says. I think that he must have a hard time, driving, or doing whatever he has to do, because now he can't use his left hand.

"It must be difficult to . . ." I say and I turn the steering wheel back and forth.

Bob looks at me like I am saying something stupid. "What do I need my hands for?" he says and he smiles at me. He is a very strange guy, this Bob.

"Segundo, like 'second,' " he says. "Who's the first, your Pop?"

"No, my brother," I say and I start to get out of the car. This Bob is asking too many questions. I just want to look at the car.

"C'mon, c'mon, scoot over," he says and starts to get in the car. I want to leave now but I move over to the passenger side anyway.

"I have a younger brother," he says. "I hate his guts."

"Why?"

"He's cheap."

"But he's your brother," I say.

"He's a person," he says. "I hate cheap people."

"Me too," I say. That is the kind of person I hate the most. You have to spend your money to get money, somebody tell me one time. That's what I'm doing with this party. A cheap person would never do this.

"I knew that, I could tell," Bob says. "You have good taste, Segundo. Not that taste and money are related. But, you know, it's really what you do with whatever you have, right?"

"Sure," I say.

He keeps on taking his candy on the stick in and out of his mouth. I don't see too many men eat candy on a stick like this. Maybe this is something they do in this country I don't know about.

"Did I mention power brakes?" he says. "Power brakes, automatic headlight dimmer. Tell me, Segundo, does your brother like cars?" he asks.

He keeps on saying my name wrong. "Secondo," I say to correct him. Then I think about the idea of Primo driving a car and it makes me laugh inside. "No, my brother, he doesn't even drive," I tell him.

"Well, some people prefer to walk," Bob says and he stares out the front window like this make him very sad.

"My brother took one ride—from Italy to America," I tell him. "I guess that's enough rides for him."

I don't know why I want to tell him about Primo but Bob looks at me like he understands what I say. But now I feel like I am all closed in the car and I have to get out. I have to go back to the booze guy. Bob holds out some keys to me.

"Let's take a test drive," he says.

"No, no, I have to go," I say.

I want to, but I look at my watch again. I still have a few minutes before Mike the booze guy is back, but I should get back because Primo is probably going crazy by now.

Bob smiles at me. "C'mon, no commitment," he says and he hands me the keys. I think, okay, this will only take a few minutes anyway and I always wanted to drive a Cadillac, so why not.

It is a beautiful day and we go driving in the town. When I drive, Bob shows me all the features in the car. He show me how the automatic light dimmers work. The headlights dim right down when you want to go from bright to regular. Power air-condition. A radio with more stations. This car drives so smooth I can't believe I'm even in a car, it's more like being in a bed with wheels on it.

I can't believe what they make in America and that if you just work very hard then anybody can buy this car. This could never happen in Italy. They don't even have cars this big in Italy. Most cars are very small. They don't have any cars at all in some parts of my country.

When I drive I try to think what it is like to drive this car every day through the town. Everyone will know that this is my car when they see it and they will know that the Paradise is a good restaurant and very popular and they will all come to the Paradise to eat every week. This is why I want to have a car like this. Everybody knows that you take good care of your business and you are a success.

When we drive back to the lot I tell Bob about Louis Prima coming to the restaurant tonight and then I have an idea. I think that maybe if Bob the Cadillac man parks this car outside the Paradise everyone who comes to the party will think I have this car, even if I don't own it yet. But I don't say this to Bob. Instead I tell him that it would be good for his business to meet Louis Prima and the guys in his band.

"So you come and you meet him and who knows?" I say. "These guys got dough, and I am interested, I mean, maybe they will be, too."

"So you are interested," Bob says.

"Very, I am very interested," I say, even though I know I will probably be in the next century before I have enough money to buy a car like this one. "So you can drive this car tonight and, you know, park it in front, so those guys will see."

Bob laughs at this. "Well, I love Louis Prima," he says.

"Eight o'clock," I say. "If you want."

We shake hands and I start to go back to Mike the booze guy. When I walk I turn around and look back at the Cadillac one more time. It is right in the sun and it is so shiny it look like it is burning bright like a big electric lamp.

Finally I get a good deal from this Mike guy and I get the booze. It was worth it to put up with Gabriella to get this deal. But I am very late to get back so I load everything in the car and I rush back to the restaurant. It's too bad I have to be back in my own piece of shit car but then I think about Louis Prima coming tonight and I think about the Cadillac parked in front of the Paradise. When I come in to the restaurant Cristiano is sweeping up the dining room before we move the tables around to make the setup for the party.

"Cristiano, go get the booze in the car," I say.

"Please, Cristiano," he say like a wise ass. "Thank you, Cristiano. That would be very nice, Cristiano."

I pay no attention to him and go into the kitchen. Primo and Phyllis are working and they look up at me when I come in. I can tell right away from their faces I am in trouble with them.

"I know, I know," I say before they can talk. "I'm sorry, I'm sorry, but I got good wine, so where are we?"

Primo just looks at me and says nothing. Phyllis smiles at me and says, "Well, I'm just finishing the eggplant. Primo showed me." Then Primo walks away to the back door.

"Where are you going?" I say. He mumbles something I can't hear and he goes outside to the back.

"What? What did he say?" I ask Phyllis. She knows too that Primo is mad about me being so late to come back.

"What took you so long?" she says and she starts to put her arms around me and hug me. "Where have you been?"

"Phyllis, please, you don't even want to know where I been," I say. "This cheap booze guy, this is the last time I use him. I'm sorry."

"I missed you," she says and she starts to kiss me on the face. But I want to break away from her because I feel bad about where I've been and I am so late and now we still have a lot of work to do. "C'mon, Phyllis," I say, "we don't have time."

She still kisses me, and then we hear the swinging door open up and there is Pascal.

"Buon giorno, tutti quanti!" he says and then he sees me with Phyllis and says, "Oh, *scusi,"* and he goes back out the door. Phyllis lets go of me and then Pascal comes right back in with a big smile on his face.

"Ah! *Amore!"* he says. "I love love!" He goes up to Phyllis. Pascal is short and he comes up only to her chest. I can see him look right at her breasts. He takes her hand and he kisses it. *"Purità! Virtuosità!"* he says. *"Immacolata!"*

Phyllis is like my brother, she does not like Pascal either, and she makes a face like she tastes something bad in her mouth. "Oh, Mr. Pascal," she says, embarrassed. She looks at me and says, "Honey, I'm going to go shopping. Do you need me for anything?" I can see in her eyes that she just wants to get away from him.

"He need you for everything," Pascal says and he laughs like hell at his joke.

"You go ahead," I say to Phyllis and I give her a kiss on the cheek. Phyllis runs out of the kitchen like it is on fire now.

"Ahh! American girls, *oy vey!"* Pascal says and he hits me on the arm. "Fucking guy, how's it going?"

He starts to look around the kitchen at all the food my brother has started to make for the party. They have done a lot of work when I was gone. There are chickens and rabbits in the marinade, a big mountain of peeled potatoes, green beans, chopped-up tomatoes. I can smell the chicken stock for *la zuppa* cooking and Primo's *ragù* on the stove.

"Looks good, looks good," he says. "Fuck, you guys are going to town! Smells good, too! Where's your brother?" He calls out, "Hey, Michelangelo! Something's burning!" and he laughs again. Then he tastes the sauce on the stove with a spoon.

"Fuck! *Una meraviglia!*" he says. "What a good goddamn chef! Michelangelo! *Dov'è sei?*"

"I think he's busy, in the back," I say. The last thing I need right now is for Primo to see Pascal. "C'mon, I'll buy you a drink, huh?"

"Sure, a little whiskey, good," Pascal says. "I think I catch a fucking cold, goddamn frog in my throat."

I take Pascal to the dining room and at the bar I take down a bottle of Scotch, the best I got, and I pour out two drinks.

"Shaping up, shaping up!" Pascal says, looking around the place. I can see that he is in a good mood now. I want to ask him what happen with that chef on fire, but then I think I just better give him his drink and get him out of here before Primo sees he is here. I have enough problems today already.

"You got everything you need?" he asks. "You need anything, you let me know. I bought a boat."

"You bought a boat?" I say.

"I bought a boat," he says. "For sailing away, into the sunset!" Pascal is always buying something else new. That's what you can do when you have enough money. He picks up his drink and he holds it out to me. "To tonight!"

"To tonight," I say to him and we clink our glasses and take a drink. Then, *madonna miseria,* just when we do that, Primo comes in.

Chapter Six

Fried Eggplant

Melanzane Fritte

Wash and dry 2 eggplants, peel them, and cut into slices about ⅜ inch thick. Do not cut them thicker than this or they will be too heavy when you cook them. Put the slices on a large tray covered with paper towels and sprinkle them with salt to bring out their juices. Leave to rest for about 30 minutes, then rinse with water and dry very well with paper towels.

Beat 2 eggs in a bowl with a little salt and pepper. Mix ½ cup freshly grated Pecorino Romano cheese and 1 cup fresh bread crumbs in another bowl. Dredge each eggplant slice in some flour, then dip in the beaten eggs, then in the bread crumbs and cheese mixture. Make sure each slice is completely coated.

Heat a good amount of vegetable oil in a frying pan until it is very hot. Put in a few eggplant slices (one layer) and fry until golden brown. Take the slices out with a slotted spoon, drain off any extra oil, and put them on a plate covered with paper towels to absorb extra oil. Then repeat until all the slices are done. Arrange the finished slices on a serving platter. Serve hot or at room temperature. Serves four to five people.

Primo

Seco say he be back in one hour. Then it become two hour and then three. I am work very hard, Cristiano is work hard, Phyllis too. We chop all the tomato, we peel the potato, clean all the chickens. I don't know where my brother have to go on the day that he want to make this big deal party. This is his party and we are do all the work. I need his help here.

Thanks to God Phyllis is here to help us. She don't know a lot about cooking but she help clean up the dining room and she help me cut up the vegetables after I show her how. I like Phyllis. I think she is good for my brother to have around. She like to have fun. I think she can help him to get calm down some and not worry so much about everything all the time.

But I am worry about her and Secondo because I think my brother is too crazy sometime to pay attention enough to Phyllis. She is still young and he is almost ten year older but sometime I think it is the other way around and she is the one who take care of him.

We work for two hour and then I tell Phyllis and Cristiano is time to take a break. Cristiano go for a walk down to the beach like he do every day when he take a break and me and Phyllis go in the backyard to the garden. There is a nice breeze come from the ocean and we have a cigarette and I am look in some recipes that my uncle give me before we leave Italia. I want to see what he make that I can make tonight for the dinner.

Phyllis has the colander of string beans in her lap and I
show her how to snap off the ends from the beans. She stop
for one second and she take some of my recipes cards and
she look at them. My uncle write these cards in Italian. Some
of these recipes he make up himself and some are very old,
they come from our family a long time ago.

"I wish I could read this," she say. "He has beautiful
handwriting."

"Yes, he is educated, my uncle Paolo," I say.

"His restaurant's in Rome?" she ask me.

"Two now," I say. "He opens a new one soon. I get a
letter from him this week."

I find a card for *caponata*. This is a appetizer that people
everywhere in Italia like to eat and is a very old recipe. It
have eggplant and peppers, tomatoes, onions, olives. You
cook for a long time in the oven and all the flavors go together.

"I love this," I say. "I make this, too."

"Let me see," Phyllis say. She take the card from me and
she try to read but she can't read the Italian. "What is it
for?"

"Is a kind of salad, with . . ."

"With cheese, ham, beets . . . ?" she ask.

"No, no, no ham," I say. "Eggplant."

"I hate eggplant," she say and she make a face. She give
the card back to me.

"I think maybe you never really taste eggplant," I say.
"You try this I make and you see if you like."

"Okay," she say and she smile at me. "I'll probably like
it if you make it."

We sit for few minute and she do the beans. I can see
she is thinking about something. I think Phyllis is smart
because she think about what she do before she do it. She
is careful. My brother is sometime no too careful. He just

jump right in the water but he no look first to see how deep it is.

"So how are you?" she ask me.

"Eh, you know," I say.

"Good," she say. I think she ask me how I am because she want me to ask her. So I ask her how she is do.

"Oh, good," she say. "I think we're fine. We're good. We're very great. He has a lot on his mind, I know, but tonight could make a real difference. It could. I mean, Louis Prima, it's so exciting."

I nod at her. I know she is think a lot about Secondo. They see each other for a year on and off but maybe he is not always so good to her. I think maybe he see some other girl on the side. I don't know who it is but I think there is somebody. I can just tell from the way he act sometime. He go off sometime in the middle of the day and he never say where he go.

"My brother is a very good cook," I say to her. "He has cooked for you, right?"

She look at me like she is surprise I would say this. "Well, no, not really," she say. "A little."

This is what I know already. But I want to make her know more about my brother.

"Too bad, he is very good," I say and I look through the recipe cards. "You know, when our father die, we go to live with our uncle above the *trattoria*, you know, his restaurant. And we both learn to cook from him. But now, Secondo no cook a lot. I think this is because he think too much about the meal, and not just about each course."

Now I look up at her. She nod and she say nothing. I think she know what I say to her. I look at my watch. We have to move on now or we never will get everything finish.

"Well, I was going to wait for him to cut the pasta, but we can't wait any longer," I say. "Come here and help me."

"But I don't know how to do that," she say.

"What is there to know?"

"Well, I'm not—"

"Phyllis," I say, "when I think I know how to cook, it never come out good."

Phyllis smile at me and we go back in the kitchen to cut the pasta. Still no Seco. We work another hour and when we are finish I show Phyllis how to cut the eggplant. Some she cut for slices to fry and some she cut for the *caponata.* Then finally Secondo come home.

I am so mad at him that when he come back I have to leave the kitchen. I can't even look at him I am so mad. I go outside to the garden and I find some parsley in the garden to use for tonight. The sun is good on my face and after I have some time in the garden I no feel so mad anymore. I think Seco was away a long time probably because he do things for the party and for the restaurant. So I go to the bar because I want to make a *caffè* and then, there I see Seco is having a drink with that animal from across the street! Now I am mad again.

"Hey, *maestro!*" Pascal say when he see me. "That fucking sauce is unbelievable!"

"What can I say?" I say to him and I go to the machine.

"Somebody get you a compliment, you say thank you," Pascal say.

So I make a big bow to him and I say, *"Grazie!"* I no want compliment from Pascal. It no mean nothing to me what he say about my cooking. From what he serve at his place he know nothing about what is good food or what is not good food.

"Prego," he say and he laugh. I look at Seco and he look like he be afraid of something. I start to make the *caffè.* I spoon the *espresso* into the handle and tap it down. I just want to make it, then leave.

"Pascal bought a boat," Seco say to me.

"Oh, that mean you gonna sail away?" I say to Pascal.

"Maybe," Pascal say. "You know, when the sun is . . . no, when the sky is red. What is that rhyme?"

"Oh yeah," my brother say. "When is the good one?"

"Red sky at morning mean it will rain outside," I say.

Seco make a little laugh at this. "What about rain inside?" he say and he give a wink to Pascal. I don't know what he mean by this.

"Huh?" I say.

"Nothing."

"No, what do you mean?" I say.

Seco laugh again. "No, you say, 'rain outside,' and I think for you to say the word 'outside' is funny."

"Why?" I say.

"Because it can't rain inside," he say.

"I didn't say 'inside,' " I say.

"I know," he say.

"I say 'outside.' "

"No, I know."

"So where is the problem?" I say and Pascal look at me and look at Secondo and he say to Seco, "Yeah, I don't get it."

Seco smile at us. "No, it's just you don't have to say 'outside' because it can't rain inside."

Then we are all quiet. I don't know what he is try to say to me. Pascal look at me and he look at Seco. I no think he understand either what Seco say about the rain.

"What the fuck?" Pascal say and I say, "I know it can't rain inside."

Secondo put up his hands. "Forget it," he say. "Forget, forget."

Then Pascal look at me. "What the fuck is he talking about?" he ask me.

"I am confused," I say.

Now Seco look like he is upset. "No, no, I make fun," he say to Pascal.

"Oh," I say. He want to make a joke of me. And in front of Pascal.

"You make fun of your brother?" Pascal say to Secondo.

"No, it was a joke," Seco say, "I make like a joke."

Pascal point to his ear. "I don't hear the joke," he say.

"Well," Secondo say. Then we are all quiet again. Seco look like he is very hot now. The drip of my *caffè* is almost stop from the machine. Now I can go.

Pascal pick up the bottle of whiskey on the bar. "Hey, let's make a toast," he say. He pour him a drink and then Seco and then he get a glass for me and pour some in. I do not want to drink with this dog.

"No for me," I say, "It's too early."

"Is never too late!" Pascal say and he laugh. He always laugh, Pascal, but is not a happy laugh. He laugh like I think the Devil in Hell probably laugh. All rough in his throat. But I take the glass from him anyway. Then Pascal hold up his glass to us.

"To tonight," he say, "when I bring together my old friend Louis Prima with my new friends. You guys are simply the best! *Salute!*"

I no believe that he say this. *"Salute,"* Seco say, and he drink his drink but he make a face like he have some pain. I look at Pascal.

"He's your friend?" I ask him.

"Who? Louis Prima?" Pascal look at me like everybody know this.

"Yeah, you know that," Seco say to me.

"No," I say.

"Yeah, I told you —"

"No, you didn't," I say. He never tell me this.

"Yes, yes, I did," he say. "You don't just remember."

"No, I would remember," I say and I look at him so mad. Of course I would remember if Pascal was why Louis Prima come tonight. I can't believe Seco right now.

"Well, I told you," Seco say and make a little laugh but I know he is lie to me.

Pascal say to me, "Hey, I know everybody, baby. There are very few people I don't know."

First my brother is late to come help make the party and then he make fun of me in front of Pascal and now he lie to me about Louis Prima. I glare at Secondo and I pick up my *caffè* and I walk away. I hear Pascal call out to me, "Hey, Primo, where you going? Let's have another!" I go out to the kitchen and I just stop and stand very still. Cristiano is there at the block and he look up at me. Then I go over to the side table. I pick up a big platter of roast red pepper we make this morning and I throw the platter hard against the swing door and it make a big crash sound and Cristiano jump and then I just walk to the back door and go out of there.

I am so mad I want to spit like a cat. I go over to see Alberto. He have no customer right now but he is happy because he just get a new barber chair. He tell me to sit in it, to see how I like. I no even hear what he say I am so mad with my brother. I sit in the chair but I no even see it. I am think about Pascal. I am very angry he is the one that is set up this party. Seco make me crazy that he want to be a friend of this mongrel dog. I know Pascal is a bad man. He will hurt us sometime. Maybe not this party but sometime I think he do something bad to us. Is better to just stay away from him like he is a animal with a disease.

I know why Seco want to be around him. He see Pascal have money to buy things. He have a nice car, he have nice clothes, he have a big place, he buy a boat.

"How is it?" Alberto asks me about his chair.

"It's stiff," I say.

"Well, that's because it's new," he say.

I can't sit still in this chair and I say, "Yeah, but, is stiff."

"What's the matter with you?" Alberto says.

I jump up from out of the chair. I go to the window and I look out across the street at Pascal's restaurant. "Did you ever eat over there?" I say to Alberto.

"Where?" he say.

"Do you know what goes on in that man's restaurant every night?" I say to him. *"Rape! Rape! The rape of cuisine! That is what goes on in that place every night!"*

I start to walk up and down in the barbershop. I am boiling like a pot with water. I grab onto the headrest from the old barber chair and I pull it off. I want to throw it out the window at Pascal's.

"But what happened?" Alberto say. I see him look at me like I am crazy.

"Please, please, please," I say to him. "His kind of people should be shot in the street like rabid dogs because if you get too close they bite you and you die. *Viatore!"* I yell out the window. "Rapist!"

I walk up and down some more. I have enough of this. I have enough of this place. I see what is happen to Seco now. He is lie to me about what he do. If this is how it is, if he is start to lie to me about what is go on, I no want to stay here no more. Then I know what I can do and I ask Alberto if I can use his phone.

"Sure, go ahead," he say. I tell him I want to call Italy and I will pay him tomorrow. He says no to worry about. He can see I am upset. He is a good friend, Alberto.

I call home on the telephone. I want to talk to my uncle and maybe he can help me know what to do. He send me a letter last week and he tell me all about the new restaurant right inside Roma. I am very proud and happy for him. The new one will be more big and have more tables and have a more big menu than the first one. In the letter he say if we no do so good here he want us to come back. He want me to cook for him at the new *trattoria*. He want Secondo to come, too.

On the phone he ask me how is everything and I tell him things no are too good right now. I tell him about the Louis Prima party, but he never hear about Louis Prima. He say he want us to start very soon at his new place, in two month. I tell him I am flatter by his offer to us, but first I must talk to my brother. I tell him we come here together and before I can say yes I have to talk to Secondo. I tell my uncle I will call him back after I talk to him.

Alberto have a customer in the chair when I am on the phone, but I know he is listen. When I hang up the phone I go over to him. I know Alberto no want me to go back to Italia. He like that I come to see him all the time. But he just look at me and he say nothing to me.

I go and sit in the old barber chair. Is not stiff like the new chair Alberto get. I am thinking about my home. I think why Secondo want to stay here in America. We are have so much trouble right now. We no have money. Maybe he want to go back, I don't know. Maybe he is tired. I have to think when to say something to him about Uncle Paolo and his offer. Then I am tired of thinking so I put one of Alberto's towel over my face and I go off to sleep.

When I am asleep I have a dream. This is a dream I have a few time before. It is when I am very young, a little boy, maybe nine, maybe ten, and me and Secondo run and run outside the *trattoria* in Frascati. The sun is out very bright and is a day in the summer. My brother is chase me, I think. Then I run to the inside of the restaurant and I go past my uncle where he is sweeping up the floor and I go up the stairs to the second floor and I look out the window down to the ground. Seco is down there. He call up to me with my name, but he sound very far away and the sound of his voice I think to be funny. He keep call and call my name.

My aunt has the tablecloth from the wash on the line to dry near the window and I reach out to the line and I take off a tablecloth and I drop it down onto Secondo. But then what is funny is the dream make a jump and then it is very strange. It is like I no am me anymore, I am now Secondo and I can see the tablecloth come down through the sky, very slow, very beautiful like a big white cloud come down on me, and the tablecloth fall on my face and cover me up and all I can see is white.

I wake up from the dream when Alberto come and pull off the white towel I put onto my face. I open my eyes and I see him stand there and he look down on me.

"You were dreaming," he says.

"Che ore sono?" I ask him. I think now it is time for me to go back to the Paradise.

Secondo

I am so stupid because I think I could not tell Primo that Pascal set up Louis Prima to come to the Paradise. Of course he will find out. But I think it would be better if he did not know this, because I know he doesn't like Pascal so much. This is why I ask Pascal not to say nothing to Primo and I didn't think Pascal would say anything.

When Pascal spilled these beans, he said was very sorry. Primo walked out of the bar and then Pascal knew what he did. "Oh, fuck, I fucked up," he said and put his head into his hands. "Seco, I'm so sorry. We had a secret. I bragged, I am a braggart! You can hit me. Go ahead, hit me."

"No, no," I said but I did want to hit him because he screws everything up now with me and my brother. But this is my own fault.

"It's fine, I'll talk to him," I told Pascal. "He'll be thanking you in a month."

We hear a big crash in the kitchen and I know right away Primo have thrown something again and Pascal look at me. I tell him I should go back to work now because we have so much to do. He says he is sorry and if I need anything at all to call him right away. I just want him to go. He already has made enough trouble for one day. But it's hard for me to get too mad at him because he is the one who is bringing Louis Prima here. He just make a mistake, that's all.

When I go to the kitchen I see a big plate of peppers is all over the floor. Cristiano looks at me.

"Will you clean this up, please?" I ask Cristiano.

Cristiano nods at me and goes to get the broom.

"Did you see where he go?" I say and Cristiano say, "To Alberto."

Fine. Let him go there and get calm down. My brother doesn't understand what we have to do to make this business work out. Sometimes you just have to do things that you never think you could do.

Primo don't know that we could just as easy go to work for Pascal and do okay. Pascal would take care of us, he would see that we are set. But I know Primo won't do that. I just hope he get back here soon. I look around in the kitchen and I see we still have a lot of work to do for tonight.

I look on the chopping block and I see the eggplant that Phyllis tell me she cut up. It is no good. I get some new eggplant and begin to slice it up. I can't believe Primo let her do this. She ruined very good eggplant.

When Phyllis come in from shopping I am very angry

and I am slicing the eggplant very hard. I am angry at myself and Primo and Pascal and everybody. Phyllis sees this and she says, "What's wrong?"

"Nothing," I say.

"What are you doing?"

"I'm cutting more eggplant," I say. I do not look at her.

"Why?"

"Because I can't use this," I say and I show her a piece of the eggplant she cut. "You see this? It's too thick."

"I hate eggplant," she says.

"Well, it's not eggplant for you, is it?" I say. "We are having a party and some of the people who come to the party like to eat eggplant and they can't have eggplant that is cut like this, it's no good."

"Well, that's how Primo said I should cut it," she says. "I'm sure it's fine."

"No, it's not fine, Phyllis," I say. I hold the piece up in front of her. "Look at this. Do you see how thick this is? Do you know what happens when I try to cook this? It's no good. You know how heavy this would be?"

Phyllis stares at me. "Well, your brother—"

"My brother was wrong, Phyllis!" I shout at her. "If he told you to cut it like this, he was wrong! You know, everybody make mistakes, Phyllis, you should know that! And you should maybe be aware that when someone gives to you advice they could be making a mistake! So next time, you should decide for yourself what it is you need to do, okay? Exactly what you want to do, and then I won't have to throw every goddamn thing away!"

I pick up the eggplant she cut and I throw it all right into the trash can and then I walk away into the storage room. I am mad like hell and I walk up and down in the room. I hear Phyllis say something and then I hear the door to the dining room swing open and shut. I go back out into the kitchen and Phyllis is gone. I call after her, but she doesn't come back.

Great. This is just great. I do a great job here. Now everybody is gone. Now I am by myself. Okay, I do it by myself. I call Cristiano to come in and I tell him to cut up more eggplant. I tell him to make it not too thick. He just nods at me and says nothing. He knows I am angry so he just starts to cut up the eggplant like I tell him.

I start to chop up some onion and still I am mad at myself about Primo and now Phyllis and of course I cut my finger with the knife. You never should use a knife in the kitchen when you are mad because you always cut yourself.

"Fuck!" I yell out with the pain, and when I look up I see a tall pretty lady in the door. She carries a vase of beautiful flowers. "Oh, hello, yes," I say. This is the flower lady from the shop where Primo go to buy the flowers. Ann, her name is Ann.

"How are you?" I say. "Please excuse my language, I cut my finger."

"Yes, I saw," Ann says and smiles at me.

Cristiano throws me a rag so I can stop the blood. I take the flowers from Ann and I say, "Oh, you pick beautiful ones today."

"Well, it's your brother who has such a good eye for color," she says.

"Yes, he know what he like," I say. I give the flowers to Cristiano and I see Ann is looking around the kitchen for Primo.

"I'm sorry, my brother is not here," I tell her. "But he will be back, don't worry."

"Oh, well, that's okay," she says, but I can see that she wants him to be here. "Well, then, I'll just get the rest."

"I will help you," I say and I tell Cristiano to come out with us. We go outside and Ann has pulled her flower van up in the back of the yard near the garden. She opens up the doors and she take out three more vases of flowers. They are very nice. One we can put on the bar and two on the dinner table. I give two of the vases to Cristiano and he takes them back inside.

"These should be what he wanted," she says. "If there's a problem, he can always call me."

"But we will see you later tonight," I say. Ann looks at me like she is confused. "The party," I say. "Primo invite you, right?"

"Oh," she says. She knows what I am talking about now, but she shakes her head and gives a little smile and she says, "Well, no, he didn't." The way she says this make me think what I knew. Primo tried to ask her this morning when he ordered the flowers but he didn't do it. I know how he gets around girls, he gets too nervous. You have to push him.

"Unbelievable," I say to Ann. "Look, *signora*, I know he want to, but sometimes he is too . . ." I point my finger to my head like I am a crazy person and Ann smiles at me again. I can see she understands what I say to her about Primo.

"You come tonight," I say. "It will be our honor."

"Thank you, but—"

"No, no, no but," I say. "Please. Eight o'clock."

She thinks about this for a minute. Then she smiles again, a very big smile. She says, "Well, all right, thank you. I'll see you then."

She goes to her car and starts up and drives away. I am glad she will come. I think this will make Primo more happy about having this party for Louis Prima. But I think I won't tell him I ask her until she comes. That way he can have a good surprise at the party.

I see a red rubber ball lying on the pavement. It reminds me of the ball we play with in Italy when we play *il calcio*. In this country they call the game soccer but not too many people play it here. I played soccer all the time when I am growing up. Everyone plays this game when you are a boy in Italia, like everyone plays baseball in this country.

I start to play with the ball, kicking it up into the air and catching it with my foot. Then I see a little boy poke his head around the corner of the building. I think him to be about eight or nine years old. He is watching me kick the ball.

"This is yours?" I ask him.

He nods at me. He is a skinny boy with freckles on his face. I throw him the ball.

"Teach me how to do that," he says.

"No, no, I am too busy," I say.

He looks up at me with big blue eyes. He is like a little cherub. "C'mon, please?"

I give him the ball and he tries to do what I do with his feet. The ball keeps going away from him. He is having a hard time trying this. I show him how to keep the ball in the air when you use the top part of your foot. Not the toes but the top. He tries again and he does it okay.

"No too bad," I say to him. "Wait right there."

I go inside to the kitchen and I take a tray of pastries we get from the bakery on the next block. They are very beautiful and there are eclairs, *sfogliatelle, cannoli.* I bring the tray out to the boy and hold it in front of his nose. His eyes get very wide open like he is going into a candy store.

"Here, take the one you like," I say. He looks at them, very serious.

"Can I have two?"

"No, only one," I say. He points to a rum ball.

"No, not that one, that has rum in it," I say. The boy looks at them, back and forth, but he can't make his mind up.

"C'mon, you have to pick something," I say. *Finalmente,*

he points at a big chocolate eclair. It is bigger than his hand. He picks it up in two hands and takes a big bite from it.

"Good, huh?" I say. He nods. He is happy. Then he looks up at me again.

"You gonna be here tomorrow?" he says. I have to laugh when he ask this. I wish I knew.

"I hope so," I say. "C'mere." I take out my handkerchief and I wipe off his mouth.

"I'll come back tomorrow," he says.

"Okay," I say and he picks up his ball and he runs off around the corner.

Then I make myself a *caffè* and I go back to the kitchen. Cristiano is working, cleaning the pasta machine we used this morning. I start to think that maybe Primo is so angry at me this time he will not come back to make the rest of the party. So I go around and check on what is done so far. The greens are cleaned and ready for the salad. The rabbit and chickens are in the marinade, and I spoon it around them some more. I feel the *timpano* dough to be sure it is still moist under the towel.

I finish my *caffè* and I stand behind the stove. I put my apron on over my head and tie it in the back. On the stove, the chicken stock for *la zuppa* is cooking, and the *sugo*, and the *fagioli* are soaking. I am thinking to myself if I can finish up cooking all this food without my brother and I know if I have to do this I can because I must do it. I do not cook so much lately because I am taking care of the business. That take all my time up. But if I have to be alone for this somehow I can get everything finish in time. Once I start to cook again I will remember what I know. And I have Cristiano to help me.

Then the kitchen doors swing open and there is Primo. He is carrying a *caffè*.

"*Ciao,*" I say to him.

"Ciao," he says, very quiet. He looks at me and he takes a sip of his *caffè*.

He starts to go around the kitchen and he looks at all the food just like I did before. The way he stops at all the food he looks to me like he is a father looking in on his children when they are sleeping. When he finishes he comes around the stove to where I am. He looks at me and I know he is come back to finish the party. I move away from the stove and he takes my place and I go around to the chopping block. I start to chop up some garlic. I see Cristiano leave the kitchen to go outside to take a break and have a cigarette.

Primo starts to cook and I keep chopping. My brother and me do not say anything to each other. We have work to do.

Chapter Seven

Roasted Peppers for Antipasto

Peperoni Arrosti

Choose 4 firm, sweet red or yellow bell peppers. Put the peppers on a pan and place under the broiler. Let them get blackened on one side, then turn the peppers with tongs to another side. You want to blacken the entire skin of each pepper so that it is easy to pull off. (Try not to pierce the skin as you will lose the pepper's juice.) Continuing turning until they get black all around. If you don't have a broiler, put the peppers in an oven at 425°F for 45 minutes until they are blackened.

Put the roasted peppers into a paper bag and close it. After about 20 minutes, when they are cool enough to handle, remove the peppers from the bag and cut them in half. Try to keep some of the juices that will come out when you cut them. Peel off the skins from the peppers and remove any seeds, ribs, or stems. Cut the peppers into medium-sized strips.

Warm 4 tablespoons of extra-virgin olive oil in a large pan. Mince 2 small cloves of garlic and add to the warm oil, along with the peppers. Cook over low heat for 5 minutes, until the garlic is just golden. Add some salt and pepper to taste and some chopped Italian parsley, if you like, and cook another minute. Serve at room temperature.

Secondo

When you make a party, the trick is to do as much in the front as you can, so when the party begins, everything is all done and you can spend the time to go around and meet all the guests and make them comfortable and talk with them.

We work very hard for two hours to get everything set up for the party. We have a big table for the *antipasti* against one wall. Then we move tables together into the middle of the restaurant to make one big table for the dinner. We cover this with a lace tablecloth we bring from Italy, from our uncle's *trattoria*.

I know it is maybe too much to do but I decide to get a piano. This is not too expensive to rent for one day and I think maybe if we have a piano then Louis Prima can play something on his trumpet with one of his guys on the piano. Also, a piano I think is very classy to have at a party in case someone knows how to play and can entertain your guests. When the piano came we put it against a wall in the corner near the big table.

We have another table for the breads and for the champagne which we put in ice in a big tub I get one time from another friend of Gabriella. Then I put candles around, not too many, and some other tables near the bar for people to sit when they have a drink and eat their appetizer. Then Ann's flowers I put behind the bar and on the dinner table and some on the *antipasti* table. Everything is very simple, very nice.

Big Night

When we are done, the Paradise never look like this before. It look beautiful, like it is a new restaurant. I think Mr. Prima and his friends and all the other guests will like our place very much, they will feel very comfortable, like they just stop off at somebody's house they know to eat dinner.

At near seven o'clock we start to get dressed. Primo puts on his chef whites and he look very handsome. I try to give him a new chef's hat I buy to wear, but he won't wear it. We do not say much to each other when we are getting dressed. I think he still is mad at me and sometimes I think it is more easy to let someone blow out their own steam until they feel better.

For tonight, I get Cristiano a special waiter's jacket. It is all white with nice buttons. He is very excited to get this and I think this make him feel like he is a real waiter now. He better be, because I can't afford to hire a real waiter for the party.

For myself I get a white dinner jacket with a bow tie. This is very elegant and simple and not too much flashy. This is how I want the Paradise to be and so this is how I want to look, too.

When we are getting dressed, I try to call Phyllis on the pay phone by the bar. I want to say I am sorry about the eggplant. But her phone just rings and rings. I think that maybe she is not coming to the party now. I am sorry about this, but I have no time to deal with her right now. I want her to be here, but if she don't want to come now, that's okay, too. Sometimes I just get upset and I yell and that's how I am and she either can deal with this or not. This is a big day for us and I don't have time to waste playing games with her.

But then the three of us start to set up the big table with plates and glasses and just when we finish I hear the front door open and there is Phyllis. She just walk in without say-

ing a word and stand there looking at us. She look like a
goddess, I don't know what other word to use. She is wearing a beautiful dress that is the color of a penny and shine
like a penny too. She have on makeup and her hair is all
around her shoulders. I think she look like a movie star.

I am surprised to see her and I don't say nothing for a
minute. Primo goes up to her and gives her a kiss on the
cheek.

"You are an angel," he says and Phyllis smiles at him.

Cristiano waves to her and she waves back and Primo
comes back to me and gives me a look. Then he takes Cristiano to the kitchen because he knows I want to be alone to
talk to her. I go up to her and for a second I don't know
what to say.

"You look beautiful," I say.

"Thank you," she says.

"I tried to call you," I say.

Phyllis gives a little nod. "I was probably in the shower,"
she says and gives me a little part of a smile.

I am not sure if I should believe this to be true, but now
it doesn't matter because she is here. I put my arm around
her back and hold her close to me for a minute. She smells
good, like flowers. She is very still, very calm and she makes
me feel a little bit calm too. I know I am stupid sometimes to
get so excited about everything but this is how I am.

She looks over the place and she says, "It looks lovely in
here."

"Thank you," I say. There is not now a lot of time before
the guests start to come and there is something else I have to
fix up before they get here.

"I have to go talk to my brother for a minute," I tell her.
She nods at me and smiles, and I think we are okay again.
"I am glad you're here," I say.

She smiles again and she goes over to the bar to make a

drink. I go into the kitchen. Primo is behind the stove stirring some beans in a pot. When he look at me, I can see he is not happy. He is still mad about this afternoon. I know how he is. He cooks everything inside him like he is a pot of sauce. It takes him a long time before he forgets about something.

"So how's everything look?" I say.

"Good, good," he says.

I pick up a dish towel because I want to open the oven to check on the *timpano* and Primo have the same idea at the same time and we almost hit our heads together bending over at the oven door. We both laugh.

"Sorry," I say. "Go ahead."

Primo opens the oven door and we bend down to look at the two *timpani* in the oven. They look like they are almost done to me.

"What do you think?" I ask him.

"More time." He sounds very annoyed.

"How much?" I ask.

"Until it's done," he says, and he stands back up and goes back to stirring in the pot. I want to explain to him about this afternoon and Pascal and why I didn't tell him that Pascal set this thing up. I just was trying to keep him from getting mad and now all I did was get him mad. And also I want to say thank you to him for coming back to finish up the cooking for the party.

"Hey, look," I say.

"Do what you want," Primo says.

"No, no," I say. He thinks I mean about the *timpano*. "I mean about before. I'm sorry."

"It's okay," Primo says and he looks in the pots on the stove, tasting them and stirring them. "We do what we have to do."

"Right," I say. "After tonight, everything will be different."

Primo looks up at me. There is something going on, I can see it in his eyes, but I don't know what it is. "I know," he says.

We look at each other for a second and then I put my arm around him and we start to hug and just when we do, the kitchen doors bang open and there is Phyllis and a tall guy with a big camera.

"Say *formaggio!*" Phyllis says and the photographer flashes his camera at us. It blinds us for a second. The photographer is a friend of Phyllis's brother who likes to take pictures on the side. He really is an insurance salesman, but Phyllis said it is good idea to have someone taking pictures because then we can put them up in the front and people can see that Louis Prima was here at the Paradise. She is smart, Phyllis.

Phyllis puts some Louis Prima songs on the record player and soon after the guests start to arrive. The first to come is Alberto and Ida. I'm not surprised they come first even though they live just down the street. They like to look everything over like they are our mother and father. Ida can't believe how nice our restaurant look. She loves all the flowers and the big table in the middle. She says it looks like it is Easter Sunday and I say that's good, say a prayer for us, because we need all the help we can get tonight.

Father O'Brien comes with Ida and Alberto and he laughs at this. He is the priest from the Catholic church in the town and I think it is a good thing to ask him to the party. I don't go to church very much but Primo likes to go sometimes and he likes Father O'Brien. I think it will make Primo more comfortable with the party to have him here. And he can say the grace before we eat.

Father O'Brien is a nice man with a big balding head and I know one thing about him, he likes to eat. He's come here to the Paradise a few times and Primo fed him almost an entire veal. No charge for him, of course. Artists and priests, no charge. And cops, but no cops are coming tonight.

Then Chubby, our vegetable seller, and his wife come. His wife is a big woman too and she makes a very big sound when she laughs. I can tell she likes to have a good time because she laughs all the time. Right away Chubby starts drinking some Scotch, and I know he will drink a lot of it because he is a big man and he have room for a lot. But I get a good deal on the booze, so what the hell.

I ask Chubby to come because he tells me he likes Louis Prima a lot and he have all his records at home. I think it is good for Louis Prima if there are people here who like his music. Chubby asks me if it's all right for him to get Louis Prima's autograph and I say, sure, I'm sure he would like that very much. But wait until after we eat, I tell him.

Then Stash shows up with two women. Of course he brings two. But I can't say nothing at this point and I tell Cristiano to set another place at the table. Stash introduces one to me, who is a big black girl who wears long red gloves and lots of beads. Her name is Lenore, she says, and when she talks she has a very fancy sound to her English, like she studied it in a school. I think she is a beautiful girl. The other girl is short with a small face and she have this big scarf that she keeps twisting around Stash. I think Stash likes this girl. She says her name is Dean, which I think is funny because it sounds to me to be a man's name. I guess she must be an artist, too.

The next to show up is Bob the Cadillac guy—and he brings two women, too! I can't believe this. I tell Cristiano to set another place. Any more and we will need to make a bigger restaurant. I don't know who these girls are, I think they are just friends of Bob. They are called Natalie, who is a blonde, and Joan, who is a brunette. Bob told me in the Cadillac lot he was married and had kids but I don't think either one of these girls is Mrs. Bob. They are young girls and they wear fancy party dresses and they laugh a lot at everything Bob says, so I guess that's why they are his friends. I wonder where he meets them. He is a fast guy, this Bob.

Bob brings the Cadillac like he said he would and when I look outside the door it is right in front. It is a black convertible with a red interior that have the top down and it looks very shiny, very rich. I think Mr. Prima and everybody will be very impressed when they see this car in front of my place.

Everyone settles into the place very nice, everyone is eating the appetizer and drinking and smoking. I am nervous about Mr. Prima arriving and Pascal is not even here yet. I call Cristiano over to me.

"Go outside and watch like a dog for Louis Prima," I tell him.

"I don't know what he looks like," Cristiano say.

"Here, he look like this," I say and I take the cover from the record album we have on the record player and I give it to him. Cristiano goes outside to wait. Then Stash comes over to me. He is wearing all black clothes like he is at a funeral and he smokes a cigarette in one of those holders like in the movies.

"Secondo, I can talk to you one minute," he say.

"Sure, sure," I say. "Come, I check the buffet."

We go over to the appetizer table. Everything looks very good. We have a beautiful platter of roasted peppers and garlic with some olive oil. There are three kind of *crostini*. A *crostino* is a little piece of bread that is broiled and it have some topping on top. We make one with goat cheese and black olive and one with mozzarella, anchovy, and tomato and then a polenta *crostini* with mushroom.

We also make a salad with white bean and rosemary and garlic and a *caponata*, a eggplant appetizer which my brother always like to make. Then some endive with salmon and capers, very nice, some *focaccia* bread with rosemary and some grilled vegetables like zucchini and peppers and red onion. And of course breadstick, bread, cracker, olives, hunks of *parmigiano* cheese, everything that is good to have for the appetizer.

I see Chubby already is loading his plate up for the second time. "Everything's great, Secondo," Chubby says to me. I want to tell him to leave something for Louis Prima but I don't say this.

"Good," I say, "have whatever you like, Chubb."

Stash stands very close to me and he takes out an envelope from his jacket. He says to me, "Secondo, look, I have some good luck."

I am seeing what appetizer we need more of. The polenta *crostini* are getting low. "You did?" I say. "Good for you, Stash."

"Yes, I sell a painting," he says, "so I wanted for you to have this. It's just something, for everything."

He gives me this envelope and I open it up and inside there are five ten-dollar bills. This is fifty dollars! This is a lot of money. Especially for Stash.

"Oh, Stash, no, no, I can't take this," I say.

"No, no, I have to do this," he says, "because you keep me alive, not just in my stomach. But in here." Then he points to his heart. "And, you invite me to this party," he says.

I am embarrassed by what he says and I don't know what to say to him.

"No, Stash, invite you to the party," I say. "You are our friend, we are having a party, so . . . I mean, look, tonight is not about money. When you eat here, it is not about money. It's about . . . you know." I think it is good of him to offer the fifty dollars. No, I can't take it, but then I think about how I can use fifty dollars. I can pay for some of this party with fifty dollars. But no, I can't take this money.

"Okay, thank you," Stash says and puts the envelope back into his jacket. Then he puts his arms around me and gives me a very big hug, like he is trying to crush me.

"Okay, okay, come on, did you try anything yet?" I say and he finally lets go of me. He is very moved, I can see. "Here, come, we get you a plate."

Then Phyllis comes up to me and whispers in my ear that a reporter is come. I go to the door and there is a very tall man in a gray suit and a hat. He have a mustache.

"I'm Jameson, *Daily Sun*," he says in a very deep voice. "Are you El Segundo?"

"Secondo," I say, "Secondo. Very nice to meet you." I shake his hand.

"Glad to know ya," he says and looks around the room. "Is Mr. Prima here?"

"Not yet," I tell him. "But we expect him any moment."

"Is Gabriella here?"

Gabriella called up this Mr. Jameson for me. I wonder if there is any man in the whole town that Gabriella does not know. In the whole state of New Jersey.

"No, but she too will be here soon," I say, leading him inside. "But please, have a drink, something to eat."

"Well, I don't know," he says.

"Please, have something," I say. "Come this way."

I take him to a booth and get him a glass of wine and I make up a little plate of appetizer for him. I want him to be very comfortable here because then he maybe will write a story in his newspaper about Louis Prima coming to the Paradise. This will make the people who read the story think we are a very popular restaurant like Pascal's where all the stars go and then we can make some money finally.

I tell Jameson the reporter about the appetizer so he will see that we make everything fresh. I explain that we make the *focaccia* this morning with rosemary and onion, and the *crostini* with goat cheese and black olives we import from Italy and the roasted red and yellow peppers. He seems to like these very much.

Jameson tells me he writes for the City Desk and he covers homicide. I don't know this word and then he tells me it means murder. I tell him I'm sure we won't have any murder here tonight, and he laughs, except maybe I'll just kill Primo if he starts to be a pain in the neck, but I don't say this to Jameson. I don't know why if he writes about murder he comes here to meet Louis Prima but I don't ask him this because I don't want him to think I don't understand. I guess any reporter is better than no reporter to come.

I hear a big laugh from Bob and one of his girls and then a wineglass hits the tile floor and breaks with a big pop sound. And there in the doorway is Ann the flower lady. She stands there and she looks very lost and shy. I say excuse me to Mr. Jameson and go over to welcome Ann to the party. I get Cristiano to clean up the glass.

"Hello, so nice you could come," I say to her. "You look beautiful." She does look very nice, in a dark blue dress and white pearls with a nice corsage that I am sure she make herself.

"Well, thank you, thank you for inviting me," she says, looking around the place.

"Please come in, you would like something, a glass of wine," I say. I lead her into the restaurant.

"All right," she says. Alberto is sitting at the bar and I tap him on the shoulder as we go by. He looks at me and I shake my head at him toward the kitchen to tell him to go and get Primo. My brother is going to get a good surprise.

Chapter Eight

Toasted Bread Appetizers

Crostini

You'll need a loaf of good Italian bread, either round (such as a country loaf) or long (baguette). The bread may either be fresh, or a day or two old, but it should be the best you can find. If using a round loaf, cut ½-inch slices, and then cut the slices in halves or in quarters, depending on the size of the loaf. If using a baguette, cut the loaf diagonally into slices about ½ inch thick.

Brush the bread slices with a good olive oil. Then either put the slices under the broiler or on a grill until they are toasted. You can also put them on a baking sheet in a 400°F oven for about 10 minutes, turning once, until they're toasted on each side.

The finished *crostini* can be topped with anything you like: roasted peppers, fresh *mozzarella* or goat cheese, black olives or olive paste, chopped fresh tomatoes, anchovies, arugula, or any combination of these.

Primo

When the guest start to come to the party I stay in the kitchen. I am think about many thing. I hear the music, and girls laughing out there and everyone is having a good time. I never hear so much laughing in our restaurant before this. I have everything ready for the meal except for what I must cook right then when the people begin to eat. I do not want to go out there right now. I let Secondo take care of them because this is what he know how to do good.

I am think about Uncle Paolo and his new *trattoria* in Roma. If I am to cook in Roma, at least there people would know what they eat and there would not be the fighting between me and Secondo all the time. Sometimes I think we try to fit in here like in a shoe that is too small and that is no good for us. People must have time to understand what I cook for them but now we have no money so I guess that mean we have no time.

Alberto come in with a glass of wine. He look very nice in his suit and tie. He ask me how I am and I say I am fine. But he know I am no so fine from what happen today. He can see this.

"Did you talk to your brother?" he say to me.

"No," I say. *Domani.*" Tomorrow.

Alberto shrug his shoulder. "Well," he say. This is what is good about Alberto, he just listen and he never tell you what to do.

I start to pick through some basil to show him I no want

to talk about this right now. He see Cristiano carry a tray of
crostini and he follow him from the kitchen to the dining
room. I watch them go and peek out through the door. There
is more laughing and joking and people are near the bar
drinking. But I don't miss this. I like to be in here.

I check on the *timpani* in the oven and I see that they are
almost done. They will take a long time to cool down before
we can eat so I turn off the oven but leave them inside. This
will give them the right time before we take them out of the
oven. Then I taste the *brodo* and think it need more salt so I
put some more in.

Then Alberto come back in the door. *"Hey, la tu'amica è
qui,"* he say and he mean my friend is here.

"Chi?" I say.

"The flower lady!" he say and go back out the door.

What? How can this be? How can she be here? I see the
flower she drop off this afternoon when I come home from
Alberto's but Secondo no say nothing about her and I no ask
him. I no want him to know that I no ask her to come to the
party tonight because I am too afraid.

I first think to take some parsley and chew on it. This
make your breath smell sweet, my uncle teach me. Then I
think I look all a sweat from the stove so I take the lid from
the stockpot and look in the lid to see myself. I fix my hair
up a little bit.

Alberto stick his head through the door one more time
and say, *"Muovi ti!"* I have to hurry up.

"I'm coming, I'm coming," I say.

Cristiano look at me and I take off my apron and throw
it at him. "Watch the stove!" I say to him and I go out the
door.

She is stand at the bar with my brother. I can't believe
she is here. I see her back only and she no see me. Then

Secondo see me and he come around the bar. I walk up to the two of them.

"Hello, big brother!" Secondo say to me. "How are you?" I want to punch him right now. He never call me this "big brother" before. Now I figure out it is him who do this. He ask her to come here. I don't know if I want to kiss him or maybe to kill him because I am too nervous to think about it.

"Hello," Ann say to me.

"Hello," I say. I never see her look so beautiful before. She is wear a dress instead of the pants she usually wear in her shop and she have a corsage on. "I am so glad you are here," I tell her. "Now you can see where go your beautiful flowers."

I wave my hand to the restaurant. It is hard to look at her because she look so good I want to cry. I want to cry too that she is here and that Secondo ask her for me and that I am such a fool for no ask her myself this morning. I am embarrass.

"Yes, see, all around, behind the bar, everywhere," Secondo say to Ann. I wish he would please shut up his mouth for one minute.

"Yes," Ann say. "It's such a lovely restaurant. I love all the paintings."

"Oh, yes," I say and shake my head.

Secondo and Ann both stare at me. "Show the lady," Secondo say and Ann say, "Will you show them to me?" and she smile at me.

"Oh, yes," I say. "Yes."

I turn around and I go to the wall near the booth. "Well, we can start here," I say. Ann come after me with her glass of wine. I show her a painting of a still life made by my aunt.

"This one my aunt make, she ask me what are the things

I like and I tell her food and music and books, so she make this with all them in there," I say. "Do you see?" I am all out of breath like I just run around a lot.

"It's lovely," Ann says. I smell the flowers in her corsage but also I smell her own smell of flowers like I did in the morning at her shop. Then I show her another one, a drawing, and after that I show her about five more. I think maybe she get tired of looking at the paintings so I ask her if she would like some appetizer. She go to sit down and I get her a plate and a plate for me because I think I better eat something so I no have to talk all the time. And I get a bottle of wine and I bring it all to a little table for us.

I can see she is nervous too like me, like we are both children in a school, but it make feel better to know she is nervous, too. I tell her about some of the appetizer and how I make.

"This is delicious," she say to me after she eat a *crostino*. "What is this called?"

"Is a *crostino*," I say. Then she says the word and I tell her her Italian is very good, better than how I talk English. She laughs at this.

Some of the people at the party begin to dance to a Louis Prima song. "*Buona sera, signorina, buona sera,* it is time to say good-bye to Napoli," he sing. We watch them dance for a minute, Secondo and Phyllis dance, and Chubby and his wife, and Stash and his friend. Some other people are here I never see before and they all start to dance too. So I think to ask Ann to dance, too.

She say yes so we start to dance. I can't believe that I am dance in our restaurant with her. I never think this would happen. I think she like me very much from the way she look at me when we dance. We dance slow first and I hold her waist with my hand, but very formal, very polite. She is tall as me but she feel very light to hold.

Then the song start to go very fast and I let go of her and we start to dance around and around and make circle and Ann laugh and laugh. I think I make her laugh because I am such a bad dancer. But I have fun anyway and I think Ann have fun, too, she laugh so much. Everything is happen so fast, I can no believe how this happen.

When we are dance Phyllis look at me and she give me a wink. I am embarrass, but I smile at her. I see she is happy for me to be with Ann. Phyllis and Secondo look like they have fun, too, I think. Even Father O'Brien dance, too. In Italia the priest never dance, but here in this country I think the priest have more fun. One thing I know, Father O'Brien like to eat my food. So I am glad he is here.

Then I think Ann is tire so we stop our dance and we sit back down in the booth again. I look over at the door and I see Pascal come in with Gabriella. Seco and Phyllis stop their dance and go to see them.

"I haven't danced like that in years," Ann say to me. We are both hot and all a sweat from dancing so I give her some more wine.

"Oh, not too much," she say. Then she pick up her glass and say, "Well, bottoms up."

"Bottoms up?" I say. I never hear this before. I don't know what this mean.

"It's a toast," she say and she hit her glass on mine. I am more confuse now but before I say something else I hear Pascal call my name and he is come toward us.

"Hey, Primo!" he yell on top of the music. I nod at him but I wish he no would come over here right now. I no want to talk to him.

"Hello, Ann!" he say when he see her and he crowd right into the booth next to Ann. He is an animal, this Pascal. He should be put in a cage. I guess he know Ann because he get flower from her too for his place. But I think if you bring a beautiful fresh flower in Pascal's restaurant it will wither and then die.

"I love your corsage," he say to her and lean over her to smell her corsage and he stick his nose right in her chest! I am embarrass for her.

"Thank you," she says and she lean back in her seat away from him. Then he whisper something in Ann's ear and she shake her head to say yes. What does he say to her? He is a *bestia*, Pascal.

Gabriella come up to us. She look beautiful like she always do but she look like she is lost here in the Paradise. "You know Gabriella?" Pascal say to me and Ann and I stand up and give a little bow to her. She shake her hand with Ann but then she turn away from us and look out at all the people dancing. I no think she want to be here very much.

Pascal lean right over Ann and say to me, "Primo, let me ask you something. You know a brand of tomato by the name of La Fortuna?"

"Sure," I say.

"What do you think?" he say.

I know this tomato. Secondo bring it to me once because he say he get a good deal. But is no good. I shake my head.

"No good," he say. "Bitter, right?"

I nod yes to him.

"That's what I knew," he say and throw his hand up. "Now I am stuck with thirty-five cases."

"How did that happen?" Ann ask.

"Well, I can't do everything myself, you know," he say. I think for one minute about this. You can't do nothing with a bad tomato.

"You should throw them out," I say.

This make Pascal laugh like I tell him a big joke. He

laugh very loud. "I love this guy!" he say to Ann. "Maybe I will, maybe I will."

Then Chubby's wife come over to say hi to Ann and I think to get out of this booth, to get out of this prison. So I say excuse me and I have to go check on the stove. Ann smiles at me and I tell her I am come back soon. I want to know from Secondo if we can start the meal now. Is start to get late.

Secondo

Everything is going pretty good at this party but still no Louis Prima. Everybody is eating all the appetizer and drinking up a storm. I tell Phyllis to put on some Louis Prima music so the guests will start dancing. She puts on *"Buona Sera"* and we start to dance to get everyone in the mood. Everyone starts to dance, even the reporter and Alberto and Ida and Father O'Brien dance with Lenore the artist. So I think everybody is having a good time so far.

Phyllis looks happy to dance with me and when we dance she whispers in my ear that she wants to go and take a walk with me later. I think she wants to go and make out with me. I tell her sure, I would like to do that, but as soon as Louis Prima comes and we get this dinner going.

When we are dancing I see Pascal and Gabriella come in the front door. Finally. Phyllis and me stop and we go over to welcome them. I think maybe Louis Prima come with him but there is just him and Gabriella.

"Hey, fucking guy!" Pascal yells over the music. "What a crowd! Here, I bring something for you."

He hands me a bottle of champagne, very nice cham-

pagne I see from the label, with a red ribbon tied on it and
he grabs me and he kisses me hard on the cheek.

"You know Gabriella, right?" he says and Gabriella and
me nod at each other. I see that Gabriella is looking over
Phyllis. Pascal stares at Phyllis, right at her chest again, like
he did in the kitchen in the afternoon.

"Phyllis, you are a vision of loveliness," he says.

"Oh, thank you," Phyllis says and smiles at him, but I
know she is embarrassed by what he says.

"Oh, yes, yes," I say.

"Phyllis, you know Gabriella?" Pascal says to introduce
them. "Phyllis, Gabriella, Gabriella, Phyllis." Then he looks
right at me and he say, "Phyllis is Secondo's . . . uh . . .
fiancée?"

"Well, no," I say and at the same time Phyllis gives a
little laugh and says, "No, not quite." Phyllis is annoyed by
this question and I see Gabriella looks like she maybe is
going to scream. Pascal makes a face like he is shocked to
hear this. But I know already he knows Phyllis and me are
not engaged. He is just playing some game with us.

"What? Secondo, what are you waiting for?" he says. "A
sign from above? C'mon!"

Then he laughs like hell and he grabs my face again and
squeezes it hard like a lemon.

"Am I right?" he says. "Am I right? I love this guy, Phyllis, I love him."

Me and Phyllis and Gabriella are too shocked to say anything more but Pascal just keeps on going. He looks at all
the dancers and past them he sees the dinner table all set up
for the meal. "So, looking good, looking good," he says.
"Would you look at that goddamn table! It's the last fucking
supper!"

He laughs like hell again and I say, "Yes, well, now we
are just waiting for the guest of honor."

"Ahh, fucking musicians, forget about it," Pascal says. "Don't worry, he'll be here! Where's your brother? I go say hi. Oh, I see him. Hey, Primo!"

Then he is off like a rocket leaving the three of us standing there. Gabriella looks at us very uncomfortable like she is going to melt into the floor. I look at the two women and I don't know what to say to them. I was hoping we would not have to have a meeting like this, the three of us by ourselves.

I look from one to the other one and start to say, "So, uh—"

"Wait, I'll come with you," Gabriella says to Pascal even though he is already at the booth where Ann and Primo are. She walks away from us. I tell Phyllis I should go into the kitchen now to check on everything and she says she is going to make herself a drink. I am glad to get us all out of there. I don't think Phyllis knows anything at all about me and Gabriella and I think I have to try and keep them away from each other tonight. This could be a disaster.

I go past Ann and Primo and I am glad I bring her here tonight. Maybe then Primo will think America is not so bad and he maybe can be not so much a pain in the neck every two minutes. I think that maybe he will like to take Ann out at night sometimes and he will not stay cooped up in his kitchen all the time like a prisoner. He makes himself a prisoner, not me. I don't make him stay there. Maybe Ann can show him around some and make him happier with the way things are here. I know I can't do it. He never listens to what I say is good for him.

Near the kitchen Bob is sitting in another booth talking to Cristiano when he is clearing a table of plates for the appetizer.

"You got everything you need?" I ask Bob.

"I'm swell," says Bob, "thanks."

"Cristiano, you take good care of my friend," I say. Cristiano nods to me.

I start to walk away and I hear Bob say, "Cristiano, right? You got a car?" This Bob is some smooth operator. I see why he came to this party tonight. I think he will probably sell a car to somebody before the night is over. At least somebody is a success around here.

When I go into the kitchen I look at everything we make that is waiting to be served for the dinner. The *timpani* are out of the oven now but they are starting to look like the time is come to serve them. The chickens look dry a little bit. I feel very tired all of a sudden and I start to think if this is a good idea, this dinner. All these people here and all this money I spend.

Primo comes in and sees me tired.

"Che c'è?" he says. What's wrong?

I shrug my shoulders. "He's not here yet, everyone is drunk out there, everything is drying out," I say and I shake my head.

"Don't worry," Primo says. "Everything will be fine, Secondo. It's a party, right? Is fun."

Oh boy. Fun. Now this is a new one to hear from my brother.

"Oh, Mr. Fun, Mr. Fun," I say to him and I throw a dish towel at him.

"Go on, I take care of this," he says and laughs at me. "Go on."

When I go back into the party I see things are starting to get a little bit crazy. The two artists who come with Stash have Cristiano in a corner and they are dressing him up with fruit and flowers. They make him pose like he is a statue holding a bottle of wine and some grapes and the short one is yelling out, "He's Bacchus! Bacchus! He's my new muse!"

The photographer is taking pictures with his flash camera and Cristiano smiles like he don't know what is going on. Everybody laughs and claps at him.

But I think Cristiano is having fun. This is good for him because Cristiano is very shy around girls. He always say he don't like girls because they make too many problems. Okay, maybe I think he is right about the problems. But I think he likes it when the short one keeps hugging him and feeding him grapes.

Over in the booth by the bar, Stash sits with his sketch pad and he is drawing Mrs. Chubby. She have a flower in her teeth and leaning against the wall like she is a statue, too. But still she is talking and laughing all the time and Stash tells her, "Don't talk!" This just makes her talk and laugh more. Things are maybe starting to get too much crazy. I am wondering about Louis Prima and where the hell is he so I go to the window to look out for him.

Phyllis stops me and says, "C'mere, honey. Give me a little kiss."

I kiss her fast and I can tell that she have a few drinks by now. She is young, Phyllis, and she can't have too many drinks or it start to make her drunk. She says, "Don't worry about everything, it'll be fine."

"I'm not worried about anything," I say but of course I am worried about everything.

"Here, have a little sip of my drink," she says and she gives me a martini and I down it all in one shot. I need this drink right now. I go to the bar and I start to clean it up a little bit. I have to do something here or I will go crazy with all this waiting.

Chubby comes over to me and he say, "Great party, Seco." He is all sweaty from dancing and his tie is almost off him. "Is there more Scotch?"

"Sure, Chubb."

I pour him a shot and then I see Pascal and Bob come past and are heading for the front door.

"Hey, where do you go?" I call after them.

"Just going to take a test drive!" Pascal call out.

"Be right back," Bob says and he jingles the car keys at me. Now I am get annoyed here. This party is starting to fall apart like a bad *lasagna.* I shove the bottle of Scotch at Chubby.

"Here, Chubb, take the bottle," I say and he looks happy about this. I go to the door and look outside and see Pascal drive Bob's car away from the curb. This is just great. Now Pascal is gone and won't be here when Louis Prima comes. I shut the door and go back inside.

I hear Phyllis talking very loud and I see she has Father O'Brien in a corner and is talking very close to his face. He looks at her like he is very concerned. I think she really drinks too much now so I go over and I want to take her away from him.

"We're not here in this room overnight," she says to him. "This has taken centuries. I mean, everything in its own time, am I right? You can't say, 'If this happens, then I will do . . . that.' I mean, you can, but if you did that all the time, then where will you be? Nowhere. Definitely safe, but probably nowhere. Because, sometimes, you just have to assume that there is water in that pool. Because you know the guy who fills it. Every year. You know the pool man. And you trust him. You have faith. And when you have faith . . . You know what I'm saying?"

I don't know and I don't think Father O'Brien knows either. She is talking crazy from too much drinking. But he nods and say, "Oh yes, you're absolutely right." Before I can pull her away from him one of Bob's girls calls out, "Hey, when do we eat?"

"Soon, soon!" I say.

Alberto is sitting right there and I say, "Where's Primo?"

"In the kitchen with Ann," he says.

"Oh, okay," I say. "Look, Alberto, do me a favor. Can you play something? To keep everybody . . . because . . ."

I look at my watch. Now it is ten o'clock and no Louis Prima yet. *Madonna miseria.*

"Sure, sure," Alberto say to me. "Whatever you want."

Alberto goes behind the bar and he takes out his mandolin. He plays so beautiful, Alberto. I hear him play last Christmas Eve after we have a dinner with him and Ida. He knows many old songs from Italy. I never hear a lot of these before, but I like them very much.

He starts to strum his mandolin and everybody crowds around him. He starts to play a song that is very quiet, very nice, a little sad. Everyone gets very quiet and listens to him. I think this is good to keep people busy while we wait. They have to do something! I think all the appetizer are almost gone.

When Alberto plays, I hear Gabriella telling Jameson the reporter about the mandolin and how this is an instrument that is very old and that many people in Italy play. Then I see Phyllis heading for the door.

"Are you all right?" I ask her.

"It's hot in here, isn't it hot in here?" she says and she wipes her brow with her hand. "I'm fine, really, I'm fine. I just want some air."

"You're sure?" I say and take her hand.

"I'm absolutely fine," she says and pulls her hand away from me and goes outside.

She seems like she is maybe angry or something, I don't know what is wrong now. She just have too many drinks.

I am going crazy now. We have to do something soon. People are getting bored waiting around to eat dinner. I don't know what we will do if Louis Prima doesn't show up here soon. We may have to eat the dinner without him. This would be just great.

Primo

Seco say we can't eat until Louis Prima come. This is fine with me. Everything is ready to go when he want. I no want anything to get too dry out so I keep basting the chicken. I have what I need to make the *risotto* all set so when is time to cook we no waste any time. You have to make the *risotto* right before you serve otherwise it is a big plate of mush.

Since we have some time I ask Ann if she want to see my kitchen. I want to show her how I cook. I know how she do her flower because I see her do them when I go to her shop. So now I want her to see how I do my work. I give her an apron to wear since we will be near the stove and I no want her to get food on her nice dress.

Ann say she never is in a restaurant kitchen before. She say she is surprise that it is not so big. You no need so much to cook good, I tell her. Just a few good pots and pans and a wooden spoon and some time.

I give her a glass of wine and she stand next to me behind the stove. I am a little bit of a show-off for her now but that is okay. I take my knife and on the board I chop some celery very fast. It is not hard to know how to chop very fast if you learn the right way. I cut my finger sometime but no too much because I know the safe way to cut. You must keep your hand always in front of the knife and you must watch very close when you chop, like a painter watch very close when he paint.

We can hear Alberto play his mandolin in the dining

room. He play very good, Alberto. He play a song I hear him play another time. Is a love song about a man who is far away from his woman and he sings about how beautiful she is and how happy he will be when he see her again.

I put the celery I chop in the pan. "See? Very simple," I say to Ann. "And then some carrot."

"Okay," she say. Ann watch me and I can see that she maybe never see someone who chop as fast as I am.

"Quick, huh?" I say. "No too fine, no too big."

"That's amazing," Ann say. "You're so fast."

"Is no very hard," I say. "Then you put all in the pan." I finish the carrot and I put it in the pan.

"What's next?" Ann say.

"Okay, next, let me see," I say. "Next, you take a taste of wine." I drink some wine and Ann laugh and drink some, too.

"Now, this is my own recipe," I say. *"Fiorentina rapido.* You know what it means, *rapido?* Fast. Quick. Rapid. It is *fiorentina* sauce, you know, but quick, fresh, nice. Sometimes you can put cream, if you like, but not for me, because that is no good for my stomach, so I no like, but some people, you know, like it."

"Oh, cream," Ann says. "My mother cooked everything with cream."

"Have you ever been to Bologna?" I ask her.

"No," Ann says.

"Oh, I take you someday there," I say. Then I see what I just say and I say, "I mean, you like cream?"

"Yes, I do," she say and she is look at me so she no see she lean her hand on the stove and it is hot. She pull her hand away because she almost burn it.

"Yes, I thought you do," I say. "You will love this place. Bologna is sad, a little, the city is old, you know, no, old is nice, but, it's dark, but the food. Ahh! They make there a

dish called *lasagna bolognese.* You can't believe how good this
is. And when my uncle, in Roma, at his restaurant, when he
make this, you eat and then you go and . . . achhh! . . . kill
yourself! You have to kill yourself!" I make like I am stab-
bing in my heart with a knife. "Because after you eat this,
you can't live!" I say.

Ann laugh at this very hard. "Now, smell," I say and I
put the pan under her nose and she smell.

"Oh, that smells so good," she says.

"Good, huh? Nice, huh?"

I taste the sauce and it is ready. "Okay, this is done,"
I tell her and I put the pan back on the stove. "Now you
taste."

Ann tries to take some sauce with her finger from the
pan but is too hot for her. I lift the pan up for her off the
stove but still is too hot for her to touch. So I take some
carrot and celery with my finger and put it to her mouth and
she take it with her lips. She taste and then she look up at
the ceiling.

"Oh, my God," she say.

"Good, huh? You like?"

"Oh, my God," she say again and she hold her hand up
to her mouth. I think she like. "Oh, my God."

"Oh my God is right!" I say to her. "Now you know. To
eat good food is to be close to God. You know what they
say? To know God, to have the . . . how do you say . . . to
have the know . . . ?" I can't think how to say this word.

"Knowledge," she say. "The knowledge?"

"Yes," I say. "The knowledge of God is the bread of
angels."

She look at me like she think about what this mean. I
hear someone say this somewhere, I no remember where.

"I never know what that mean," I say, "but I think it
sound good anyway."

She laugh at this and I laugh too and we drink some more wine. Now I think to show her how I make some *risotto*.

Secondo

Alberto plays three songs and I tell him that is enough. He is good but he is putting everybody to sleep and the people are getting bored. They walk around looking at the paintings on the wall or they sit in the booths staring at their drinks. One of Bob's girls is sitting by herself and yawning and Father O'Brien looks like he wants to go to sleep. The photographer is at the bar talking to Jameson the reporter. Bob and Pascal are still out in the car. The appetizer are gone and now it is past ten-thirty and I know people want to eat their dinner by now.

Chubby is not tired though and he puts a record on the player. He starts to mouth the words of this song into a wine bottle like it is a microphone. He is a little bit drunk, Chubby. In this song, a lady sings about a girl who goes back to Napoli and then the beat starts to get faster and Chubby begins to dance. "Hey, mambo! Mambo Italiano!" the song goes and Chubby starts to move his big body around like an elephant and he starts to dance like he is on a stage.

When they see this, everybody looks up and watches him and they begin to clap along and laugh. Then the girl who was yawning starts to sing the song too and she gets up and starts to dance behind Chubby. He goes down past the appetizer table and then Mrs. Chubby gets behind the girl and they form a line and they all dance like a conga line. This is just what I need right now.

I go to look out of the window to see if I see Louis Prima coming or even Pascal and Bob and then I see Phyllis is lying on the bench on the stoop. I go outside and say, "Phyllis, what are you doing?" Then I look up and I see Gabriella is standing right there and smoking a cigarette.

"Oh, Gabriella, hi, what is . . . ?" I say and I look from one to the other one. What are they do out here together? I think they must have been talking to each other. This is great. Phyllis looks like she is sick and Gabriella looks like she wants to be somewhere else. I don't know what to say and they both look at me but they don't say nothing.

Then we all hear a loud BEEEP! BEEEP! and Bob's Cadillac comes screeching up to the curb. Pascal is driving the car and when he stops it he lets out a big yell.

"Love me tender!" he screams. "What a fucking ride!"

Bob is laughing and then Pascal climbs right over the front seat and across the backseat and he jumps out of the car on the sidewalk. He screams again and throws his hands up to the sky. He jumps up and down like a little boy and starts waving his arms to us. I think he is like a crazy man.

"Gabriella, look at these seats!" he yells to her. "Touch them! Touch those seats! Phyllis, look! Touch!"

Phyllis sits up on the bench and gives a weak smile. Gabriella walks over to the car. She looks bored by this and is not excited like Pascal. She looks at Pascal like she doesn't think he is very funny.

"Yes, it's a beauty," I say to Pascal. Bob gets out of the car and comes over to me.

"You're still interested, right, Secondo?" he asks.

"Well, we'll have to see," I say.

Pascal hears me and he comes over. "Don't listen to him!" Pascal says. "Of course he's interested!" He puts his arm around my neck and he squeezes it hard. "I love this fucking guy!" he says to everyone. Then he says to me, "Is Louis here yet?"

"Well, no," I say and put my hands up to him like to say

I would be happy if Mr. Prima was here now. Shit, it now is almost eleven o'clock. Where is he? I know musicians can play late sometimes but Pascal says that tonight is the night off for Louis Prima and his band.

"What?" Pascal says. "Where's the phone? C'mon, Bobby, let's go get a drink."

He leads the way inside the restaurant and everybody else follows him. I am glad that he will call Louis Prima now so we can get this dinner served. This is crazy! I want to ask Phyllis if she is okay now but when we go inside the restaurant it is like a crazy house. It looks like a *carnevale* is going on here. People are going crazy with this song "Mambo Italiano," and it is now very loud. Everybody is in a big line and they are going all around the restaurant like a big snake. Chubby is in the front and Father O'Brien is in the back and in the middle is everybody else. Even Ida and Alberto are dancing in the line like they are *bambini!*

I see Phyllis and Gabriella see this and now look at each other like they are new best friends. *Madonna miseria.* They get in the line and go dancing around with everybody else. They are all singing and some people are screaming and carrying chairs with them and wine bottles and food. They go all the way around the table and past the bar and down to the bathroom in the hallway and then they come back and keep going around.

Pascal and Bob get a drink from the bar and Pascal gets on the phone and is yelling above the music.

"Louis Prima!" he shouts into the phone and then to me he yells, "He's not there, but I'm leaving a message for him at his hotel!"

"My name is Pascal," he says into the phone. "What's your name?"

I can't hear really what he says next because of the music but then something must happen on the other end of the phone because he throws the receiver down, picks up his drink and takes a shot and grabs Bob and they get on the dancing line, too. Everybody is whooping it up like crazy and I guess this is good because everybody is happy and having a good fun time. But this is not why I ask people to come here, to dance around like nuts. And now Pascal can't even find Louis Prima. Great.

Finally the song comes to the end and everybody stops right around the dinner table and they all clap and cheer and holler very loud. Everyone is sweating and laughing and breathing hard and I see Father O'Brien look through the pass-through window into the kitchen. Then he turns back to the crowd and yells out, "Hey, Primo's cooking!"

Everybody cheers again and they all run to the kitchen doors and push them open. I run too and push through the crowd and when I get to the door I see Primo and Ann are behind the stove. They look surprised like somebody is shining a big spotlight on them. Primo is making a stupid smile and Ann looks very embarrassed to see all the people staring at them.

I look at Primo and Primo looks at me like he wants to know is it time to eat now or what. I turn around and look at Pascal. He just stares at me. I think he will say something to me about holding up the dinner some more time for Louis Prima, but he says nothing. I think for a minute and everyone is looking at me and waiting. We better do this right now so I say, "Let's eat!"

Everybody gives out a big yell and claps. So, here we go.

Chapter Nine

Roast Chicken

Pollo Arrosto

Get the very best whole cleaned chicken, about 3 pounds, from your butcher. Wash and dry the chicken. Peel three cloves of garlic and put them into the cavity of the chicken, along with a half teaspoon of fresh (or dried) rosemary. Add some salt and a few grindings of fresh pepper.

Rub 2 tablespoons of vegetable oil or butter all over the chicken, sprinkle on some salt, pepper, and rosemary to taste. Add 2 more tablespoons of oil to a roasting pan and put in the chicken, breast down. Cook on the middle rack of a preheated 375°F oven for 30 minutes, basting after 15 minutes or so with the fat and juices at the bottom of the pan. After 30 minutes, remove the pan from the oven and turn the chicken over onto its back and baste again, and then roast for another 35 to 45 minutes, basting once more. The chicken is done when the skin is crisp and browned or when the juices that run from the cavity are clear.

Take the chicken from the oven, put it on a platter, and allow it to rest for 15 minutes before serving. If you want to serve juices with the chicken, spoon almost all the fat from the pan, put the pan on top of the stove, add 2 tablespoons of water, and over medium heat, scrape any browned bits with a wooden spoon as the water boils away. Serves 4 people.

Secondo

First I show everybody where to sit at the big table. We leave the four places at the end of the table near the kitchen empty for when Louis Prima gets here. I don't know how many people he will bring with him but I don't think it can be more than four. If it is, we will make everybody move or we will squeeze in the extra where we can fit. I don't care if he brings a whole bus of people with him. At this point I just want him to come.

I put Stash on the other head of the table because I think he is the artist like Louis Prima and he should have the second place of honor at this table. Next to him on his left hand side is Ann, then Pascal, then Ida, so she can talk in Italian to him if she wants to, then Chubby, then Phyllis, then Chubby's wife and then the photographer (I still don't know his name and he doesn't talk too much) and last at the end Father O'Brien.

On the other side Bob's girl Natalie sits next to the artist who calls herself Lenore. Then comes the reporter, Mr. Jameson, then Gabriella because she knows him and can explain what all the food is to him, then Bob and his other girl Joan, and then the other artist who calls herself Dean (she is the short one) and then Alberto because I think he will make Louis Prima feel right at home and he can talk to him in Italian. I know Louis Prima talks in Italian from his records.

I think we do a good job with the table because it looks

beautiful. We have candles in the middle and I light them
and turn off the lights by the bar to change the mood of the
room. Everyone is more calm now and I think even though
they eat up all the appetizer they are hungry now from all
that dancing around. Besides, I think Chubby ate most of
the appetizer by himself.

Cristiano and myself start to pour the wine. I am serving
only a red *chianti classico* with this dinner because I think it
is too much to have both the red and the white wines. This
is a very good wine, nice and dry, and I get a good deal on
three cases from Mike, so we will have plenty of wine for
the meal. Then on the table we have the bottles of *acqua
minerale* for the people to drink instead of the water from the
tap. I have to import this myself because nobody sells this
around where we are. Nobody around here really knows
about this water except Stash. In Italy everybody drinks this
all the time at the table. When we finish with pouring out
the wine, I open the door to the kitchen to get Primo.

"Primo, *andiamo*," I tell him. He takes off his apron and
he comes out. "You want to say something?" I ask him.

"*Io?* No," he say. "You."

"Okay," I say and I go to the head of the table where
Louis Prima will sit when he gets here. I look out at everyone around the table and smile. Everybody smiles back at
me like they are very happy to be here and this makes me
glad.

"My brother and I are happy for everyone to be here,
thank you," I say, "to enjoy this food, our food, we make.
Tonight we serve to you dishes that come from our region,
from our family, and from inside our heads. We hope you
enjoy them because it is maybe different than what you think
to find."

Everyone laughs when I say this because they know we
sometimes have trouble with our customers when they don't

know what is a *risotto* or a *pesto*. I look at my watch and now it is after eleven.

To finish my welcome talk I say, "So, I hope that Louis Prima . . . well, I hope he come so he has the chance to eat with all of you. Thank you."

Everyone claps.

"Okay, now Father O'Brien will say the grace," I say.

Father O'Brien stands up. I think he is tired from waiting around all the night for his big moment. He asks everyone to bow down their heads and to pray for God's blessing. He closes his eyes and he folds his hands together and he says, "Father in Heaven, bless this food we are about to eat, and all of us gathered here tonight. We ask you to watch over our friends Primo and Secondo, who have given so generously of themselves so that we may honor you with this meal."

He makes a pause. Everyone is quiet. Then he says, "And we also ask a special blessing for Mr. Louis Prima, wherever the hell he may be." Everyone laughs at his joke. "In Jesus Christ's name, amen."

"Amen," everybody says and Pascal picks up his glass and he says to the table, *"Buon appetito, tutti."*

Everybody answers him and I give Cristiano the sign that we can now serve the soup. We go to the kitchen and we get the soup tureens that Primo is made ready. We take these to the table and we ladle the soup into each person's bowl in front of them. You never bring the soup from the kitchen already in the person's bowl. That is how I see they do it here in this country but I think this is very bad service.

In Italy people eat in a very different way than here in America. I know here people are too busy to spend so much time at the dinner table but in Italy this is not how you eat. First of all, in Italy you eat the big meal of your day in the middle of the day, not at night. For two hours in the afternoon, everything just shuts right down. You eat and you take a little rest and then you can go back to your work. I know here people cannot do this and they like to eat their big meal when they come home from work. But I think it is better for your stomach to eat the most food during the daytime.

Another thing that is different is that here people have the pasta just for the whole meal. In Italy, the pasta is just one of the courses in the meal. Most times you have two courses, a soup or a pasta or a *risotto* for the first, so this is called *i primi*. And then you have *i secondi*, and for this there is a meat or fish with vegetables on the side. And then some *dolce* and *caffè*. You probably figure out that my brother and me get our names Primo and Secondo from these names for the courses in the meal. Also because Primo came first and I came second.

Because this dinner for Louis Prima is a big deal, a *festa*, Primo wants to have more courses than two. We already have the *antipasti*, the appetizer, during the party. So we start the dinner with *la zuppa*, the soup. For *la zuppa*, Primo make a nice *garganelli con brodo*. A *garganello* is a kind of pasta that is like a *ziti* or *penne* but you make it in a special way. You take the square of the pasta dough that you make already and you have a special stick that you use to roll on the dough and make it into a tube. You have to make each one at a time. Then Primo cook the *garganelli* in a nice chicken broth, very simple, with some carrot and celery and onion. It is delicious.

The guests start to eat the soup and Cristiano and myself stand to the side in the case that somebody ask for more. Everybody is very quiet when they eat the soup because I think they never have a soup that tastes like this before here in America. Then I start to hear people make a moan sound as they finish. Bob makes a big sound and I see Chubby's wife close her eyes every time she takes a spoon in her mouth.

Everyone puts down their spoons in the bowls and it makes a clatter sound and from the way they look I think that maybe they are happy just having this soup and don't need anything else. But we have so much more to serve to them.

Cristiano and myself pick up the empty bowls now and we carry them into the kitchen. When we go in Primo looks at us like he is saying *how do they like?* We smile and nod at him and take the bowls to the sink. I give Primo a little slap on his back to say that *la zuppa* was a very good start to the meal. Primo smiles and he looks very happy that people like his soup so much.

When I go back out to the table I hear Alberto talking to the artist Dean. He says, "This lady say to me, 'My great-great-great-grandfather come over to here on the ship called the *Mayflower.*' And I say, 'Oh really? That's funny, because my great-great-great-great-grandfather come here on a ship, too. It was called the *Santa Maria!*' These people! Think America belong to them."

I am starting to serve the *risotto* and I think it is funny that this young woman from America is sitting with this old man who comes from another time and another place and they are starting to be friends. I like when this happen at a dinner table because it show that when you sit and eat good food together, everyone can be okay with each other no matter where you come from.

For the first *i primi* course, Primo make *risotto* in three different kinds, one green, one white, one red. These are the colors of the Italian flag. The green is a *pesto risotto*, made with the basil *pesto* that come from the Liguria region, the red is a seafood *risotto*, and the white is a regular *risotto*. We put each one on platter to make three stripes and it looks beautiful.

Cristiano serves one platter to one side of the table and I serve to the other. This is the first time Cristiano serves at the table and I have to watch my eye on him to make sure he does it right. He has seen me serve *risotto* to customers many times and he knows what to do.

I start to serve Stash first and then Ann. When I serve her, I tell her that the green one my brother has made especially for her because it is the color of the plants she sells. She blushes all red when I say this.

Then I reach Pascal and ask him which one he likes and he says he wants a little bit of each.

"Can I come back for more?" he asks when I serve him and I say no and everyone laughs. Then I bend down and talk down low to him so no one will hear us.

"Do you think he will make it?" I ask.

"Who, Louis Prima?" he says. "He better make it. He don't know what he's missing."

This doesn't make me feel too good, but what can I do? I have to keep on serving the *risotto* to the other guests. Chubby of course wants practically the whole platter and then next comes Phyllis.

Before when we were in the kitchen and we were waiting for Primo to finish making the *risotto*, Cristiano told me Phyllis was sick in the flowerpots outside in the front of the restaurant. This was after she said she needed to go outside and get some air. He went outside too to look for Louis Prima again and he saw Gabriella taking care of Phyllis. She gave Phyllis a handkerchief and then they smoked a cigarette and they talked. So that is what they were doing out there when I found them.

"What did they say?" I asked Cristiano. He always seems to know what everybody says. This is because he is around all the time and he doesn't say too much, he just listens. I want to know if they said something about me.

"Gabriella says she wants to have a cowboy," Cristiano said.

"A cowboy?" I said.

Cristiano said he heard Gabriella ask Phyllis if she had ever gone out to the West because they say it is very beautiful. Phyllis said it was but that it was too vast for her. Gabriella did not know this word, "vast," and Cristiano said he did not know this word either. Then Phyllis said "vast" means big. Then Gabriella said maybe she wanted to go out to the West and get a cowboy with a horse for herself, that she wanted one because cowboys are strong and silent and they are always there, like a statue. Phyllis laughed at this and Cristiano said he could see she felt much better after this and he didn't see Louis Prima coming anywhere so he went back inside.

Why does Gabriella want a cowboy? What is she talking about? And why did Phyllis feel okay after she said this? I don't understand these women.

"How are you doing?" I say to Phyllis when I get to her with the *risotto*.

"I'm fine, I'm fine, I'm absolutely fine," she says. "I should be helping you."

"No, no," I say. I see that she is not fine. Her face is all pale. I feel bad that she got sick and I didn't know. Everything just got so crazy with Pascal and Bob coming back in the car and the mambo dancing and then the dinner starting and I haven't even had one minute to talk to her.

I want to give her some *risotto* but she says she doesn't want any. I give her a little kiss on the cheek and when I look up, I see Gabriella is watching us. She is smiling and when I go to serve Mrs. Chubby next I can feel that Gabriella is still watching me. Now, though, she is smiling at me.

I think she maybe did not realize that I know how to run this restaurant and serve like a good waiter and do it all. I think maybe she is impressed.

From the outside of my eye I see Pascal throw a cork from the wine bottle at Gabriella and he laugh to himself. He is like a little boy in school, Pascal. She looks around but she doesn't know who threw the cork at her. This makes me very nervous because now I think Pascal maybe know something about me and Gabriella. But maybe I am just nervous about the whole dinner anyway and he is just playing the games he plays all the time with her.

Gabriella tells me they play tricks on each other all the time. One time Pascal was getting dressed in his room and Gabriella sneaked in the door and crawled on the floor up behind him and surprised him from his behind and Pascal screamed but then he started to laugh so hard. I told her not to tell me any more stories about how she has fun with Pascal. She just laughed at me and called me a *bambino*, which means a baby boy in Italian. But now I think, maybe, she will think about me in a different way after this dinner. She will see what it means to do some work, maybe.

When I get to the end of the table and everyone is served I look back over and everyone is eating the *risotto*. Everyone seems to like it very much but I see Dean the artist pushing it around on her plate.

"Taste it, taste it, you'll like it," Alberto says to her.

"What is this?" she asks him.

I think she doesn't know what is a *risotto*. I watch her as she puts some in her mouth and tastes. She closes her eyes like someone is kissing her.

"This is wonderful!" she says. "What's this called?"

"*Risotto*," Alberto says.

"*Ri-sot-to*," Dean says.

"It means rice in Italian," says Alberto.

"This stuff is rice?" she says. "It tastes like a dream!"

I know this will make Primo feel good that everyone is eating his *risotto*. Now if we can just get everyone in the whole town to come in and try some *risotto* we'll have some good business. Without Louis Prima I don't know how we can do that now.

Primo

I am happy everyone like the soup I make. I think to make the *garganelli con brodo* because this is very light soup, not too heavy to start the meal, and I think people can understand what is a *brodo*, it is simple and everyone like this everywhere. Is just good chicken soup with some pasta in it.

Then the *risotto*. I make three different kind because maybe if someone no like one kind they can have another kind. *Risotto* is like pasta because you can make so many way and there is always one way somebody like. You can make with seafood, with mushroom, with vegetable, many way. But I am nervous because I know that some people in this country are confuse by a *risotto*.

Cristiano come into the kitchen with some dirty dish from the *risotto*.

"Do they like?" I say.

Cristiano stop and he smile at me. "I think they are in love," he say and he go to the sink with the dish. Then Secondo come in with some dirty dish too. He put them in the sink and he stop and mop his brow with his handkerchief. Is hard work to serve the *risotto* to so many people at the same time. I know it has been a long time since he have to do this to a big crowd like this.

"Okay," he say to me. "He missed the soup and he

missed the *risotto*, which everyone is having a heart attack over."

"Oh, so they like the *risotto*," I say. I can't stop myself from saying this. I show him that people can like *risotto* in this country. They just need the time to try and get use to it.

"Okay, okay," he say. "What do you think? Should we go on?"

I want to go on but I say it is up to him to decide. I know he want Louis Prima to be here but now all I think about is the meal. We already begin and you can't just stop the meal in the middle. This is like to stop in the middle when you make love with a woman.

"Okay, let's go," Seco say. This mean now is time for the *timpano*.

We go to the big board where I put the *timpano* to cool off from the oven. It take a few hour to cool off before you can take out of the tub. You must be very careful when you take this from the tub because it can all fall apart if it is too hot.

We turn over the first tub very careful and put it on the board. I hit the tub with my hand very soft to loosen it up and then Seco grab the sides and he lift off the tub.

This *timpano* look beautiful. The pastry is golden brown on the outside the way I like it to be. My uncle teach me how to make this come out and look good on the outside. What is hard to do is make sure the inside is all cook all the way through without making the outside burn and look black.

I go to get the other tub with the *timpano* we make but Seco stop me. "No, save this one for Louis Prima," he say.

My brother and me look over the *timpano* on the board. We no make *timpano* in a long time and now we have a whole table of guest waiting to eat. Cristiano stand behind us and watch. He try to touch the *timpano* but we hit his hand away.

I tap the side of the *timpano* and it feel good. Secondo tap too. He look at me and I nod again. Then we lean down and put our ear on the side to hear the inside of the *timpano*. I see my uncle do this but I'm not sure what I should hear in there. But it make me feel better to do this. I can feel the heat from the inside and it still feel very hot.

"Maybe too hot still," I say.

"Well, we have to serve now," Secondo say and he point out at the dining room.

"I know, I know."

I think okay, we can try to cut a piece to see if this is too hot and I pick up the knife but before I cut Secondo grab my arm.

"No, wait!" he say. "Cut at the table!"

"Okay," I say.

"Okay!"

I hear him breathe next to me. He look nervous, too. We start to slide the board off the table to carry the *timpano* to the dining room and Secondo say, "I hope it's not too hot, it will fall apart!"

"That's what I say, is too hot," I say and start to push the board back on the table but Secondo say, "No, we don't have time for too hot, let's go! Cristiano, open the door!"

Cristiano hold open the door and we carry the board to the table. Everyone at the table is talking and drinking wine and laughing. Some stop and look at us with the *timpano*.

"What is that?" I hear this young girl say to Stash.

"It's *timpano*," he say. "It's a special recipe they bring from their hometown. I have only heard about this, I've never had it."

"Is it a cake?" I hear the girl say. *Dio mio.*

I cut in the *timpano* with the knife two times and pull out the first piece. It is all okay, thanks to God. It is beautiful and everyone make a big sound when they see the first slice.

Big Night

Inside the timpano there is *ziti* pasta, slice of eggs that are hard boil, some salami, and provolone cheese and little meatballs and marinara sauce, and everything is hold together with a pastry crust. You can have other kind of food in a *timpano* but this is how my uncle show me to make.

Sometimes my uncle and aunt and other people in the family have a fight about how to make the *timpano*. Everybody have an idea about what to put in, when to put in, how long to cook the pasta before you bake (if you cook too much, the pasta get like mush in the *timpano*), how much cheese to put in and like that. Is a fun kind of fight, though, no very serious.

This is because the *timpano* is fill with more than just this food or that food. I think it is fill with what people think about what is food and what food they like to eat or no eat or how they like to cook or no cook. So is more than just a pasta, the *timpano*.

We make a plate of *timpano* for everyone and when they start to eat I think they like it very much. They make sounds like it is good. Everyone at the table is talk about the *timpano* and say they never see anything like this and isn't this delicious. Mrs. Chubby say she want me to give to her the recipe for the *timpano* but I say I can't do this because the *timpano* is a recipe from my family, very old, and is like a secret.

Everyone is having a good time eating the *timpano* and then all in a sudden Pascal make a big BANG on the table with his fist and all the glass on the table make a noise and everybody jump right out of their seat.

"*Goddamnit!*" Pascal scream. "*Goddamnit! I should kill you!*"

I look over at Secondo. He look worried and I look at Gabriella and I see her look at Secondo. Pascal jump up from his chair and I think he will go to Secondo but he come over to me. He look like he is very mad at me.

Everyone at the table is quiet and look at us. Secondo walk toward me and stop. Pascal look up at me and he put his hands on my shoulders. He say to me, "This is so fucking good I should kill you!"

He throw his arm around me and give me a big hug. I start to laugh, he is so crazy, Pascal, and everyone else start to laugh too. Pascal pick up a glass of wine from the table and he hold it out to the table.

"Paradise!" he say and everyone pick up their glass and they make a toast to me and my brother. I feel good that everyone like what we do. I think this is the first time I feel this way since we come to America. Secondo come over and he hold his hand up to me like I am the one who did all this. Everyone clap for me. I am embarrass but it feel good at the same time.

Then I hear Ida say, "Who's that?" and Chubby's wife say, "Oh, is that him?" and she point at the door. Everyone turn and look at the front door to the Paradise. There is a man stand there in the dark and I can't see who it is. Secondo start to walk to the door and the man come into the light.

This man is not Louis Prima. I know who is this guy, he is Leo, the guy who work for Pascal. I think he is an animal like Pascal, but Leo is like a big animal, like a big gorilla. He have on a tuxedo and he look around at the table to find Pascal. Pascal nod at him but he no say nothing. No one at the table say nothing, either. Leo walk over to near Pascal.

"Hey, yeah, how you doin'?" he say to everybody. I no think he is too smart, this Leo. He work for Pascal but I think he is scare of him.

Leo look right at Pascal and he say, "Yeah, there's a little ... uh ... we got a little problem. . . . It's just that Frankie ... uh ... Frankie the chef is sick and uh ... I mean he's got the runs, and he says he needs to go home, and I mean

Phil can take over for him . . . you know, he's there . . . and it's slowing down anyway . . . so I figured I'd let Frankie go because he's got the runs and Phil probably knows what he doing, so . . . I just wanted to check with you on . . . you know . . . that."

Everyone's eyes are on Leo. Pascal just stare at Leo and say nothing. Leo put his finger in his collar and pull it out from his neck like it is too tight on him. He nod his head up and down like a stupid gorilla.

"Yeah, okay, so I'm just gonna let him go . . . I'm gonna let him go home," he say. "All right. That's what I figured. All right." Pascal just blink at him. Then Leo turn to everyone at the table and say, "Hey, looks like a good party. Okay, I'll see you later." He wave his hand and he turn to walk away and he hit into the barstool at the bar and knock it over and then he pick it up and wave again and walk out the door.

No one say nothing for a second. One of Bob's girls start to laugh and then other people laugh and look at Pascal and then Pascal start to laugh and soon he is laughing the most hard. I am laugh, too. Secondo no laugh because I think he want it to be Louis Prima and is no Louis Prima. Just stupid Leo.

Everyone go back to eat their *timpano* and we go back in the kitchen. Now I have the real work to do because now come the time in the dinner when we start to serve *i secondi.*

Secondo

The *timpano* makes a big hit. I hate to say that Primo is right about serving the *timpano* but he is right. No one ever heard of this before and it taste so goddamn good people can hardly believe it. It's a funny thing about the *timpano* because is nothing really more than a pasta inside a pastry shell. But

I think these people are used to eating spaghetti and meat-balls and maybe sometimes a *lasagna* and that is it. Also the *timpano* makes a big splash when you bring it out to the table. It is big like a soccer ball and then when you cut it, it have surprises inside that you don't think you will have with your pasta.

Pascal scared me when he banged on the table and he screamed "*I should kill you!*" during the *timpano* course. Of course I thought right away that he meant me because he found out about me and Gabriella. I saw Gabriella was scared too because she looked at me when Pascal got up from his chair. But then he went to Primo and said that the *timpano* was so good he wanted to kill Primo. He was only making a joke. Some joke. He scared the hell from me. But I just smiled and laughed with everybody else at him.

Pascal acts like a crazy man and the funny part is that he can get away with this whenever he wants to. Because even though he acts crazy sometimes he makes people feel good too. I think he is an okay guy although then I remember the chef on fire and I don't know.

Cristiano and I wait until everyone is finished with the *timpano* and then we clear off the plates from the table. Everybody is much more awake now than when we started. Everybody is talking to everybody else and laughing and telling jokes and saying how much they like the food we serve.

I see Cristiano talking to Father O'Brien when he is pouring out some wine and then the bottle is empty. He comes up to me and says, "Seco, we are out of wine."

"So go open more wine," I say. "You are the waiter."

Cristiano's face gets very happy when I say this. He's never opened the wine before because I never let him. He nods and he goes into the kitchen to get some more wine.

I take the *timpano* plates into the kitchen and put them in

the sink. Primo is sautéing some grapes with some onions.
He tells me to get the chickens out from the oven and start
to make the platters.

I take out the first pan of chickens. These are very sweet
chickens we get from a farm not too far away from here.
Primo cooks them very simple, very easy. He puts garlic and
fresh rosemary inside the chicken with some salt and fresh
pepper and then rubs the outside with oil and some more
salt and pepper. Then he roasts in the oven and he bastes
with the juice from the chicken once in a while. You cook
until the skin get very brown and crisp. This all you need to
do with a chicken. Of course you can cook chicken many
other ways but I like this the best. I set up the chickens with
some greens and some lemons on the platters. We will carve
at the table to serve one half to each person.

For *i secondi* you usually have one meat and then some
vegetables to go with it. But because this is a big party we
make more than just these chickens. Primo roast the whole
salmon we get this morning in the oven with herbs from the
garden. I put this on a platter and he will fillet this at the
table too. When you watch Primo fillet the fish is like watching a doctor who does surgery. He know exactly how to take
the fish apart without getting the bones in everywhere.

Then he also make a braised rabbit because he knows
Stash likes this dish very much. This tastes a little bit like a
chicken and a little like a veal. It is a very sweet meat and he
cooks this in some white wine, rosemary, garlic, and a little
tomato. We serve this on a bed of polenta and mushroom.
No wonder Stash likes this. You have to be dead not to like
this.

Primo also wants to have a veal dish. I get some very
nice veal from the butcher in the next town who is Italian
and who knows what is a good veal, not like what I see in
places like Pascal's. This he flattens out and he puts in a

layer of *pancetta*, which is a kind of bacon we get from Italy and then he cooks this in white wine and garlic. This is already done and I take the veal to the cutting board and slice it up and put on a platter too. Primo take the drippings from the pan and pours it on top.

To go with *i secondi* we make four different kinds of *le verdure*. Usually you just have one or two vegetables but we need more to go with the chicken and fish and veal and rabbit. So we make some potatoes roasted in the pan with olive oil, some fresh artichokes we cook *alla romana* with lemon, parsley, garlic, and mint, and green beans with red pepper and some tomato and a platter of carrots cooked very slow with butter and then *parmigiano* cheese on top. And then the grapes and baby onions Primo cook together.

To make all this ready at the same time we must move very fast. It has been some time since Primo and me cook together so many dishes at once. When we cook together we don't have to say very much to each other. We don't fight very much like we usually do. When we cook together we know what the other one is doing and what have to come next. When I am dressing the fish with herbs, he is tasting the potatoes to be sure there is enough salt.

I call Cristiano from the dining room to come help us and we start to take out the platters of food. Except maybe for Alberto and Ida and Gabriella I don't think anybody has ever seen this much food come to one table all at the same time. Nobody can believe we make all this by ourselves.

"There's more?" Lenore the artist says when she sees all this food come out.

"Oh, yeah!" Chubby says. He looks like he just died and woke up with the angels.

We get everyone set up with a plate with whatever they like. Chubby has the most, of course, and Father O'Brien has a lot, too. Everybody has a full plate except for Phyllis.

I don't think she feels too good still. I tell her to have a little piece of chicken because it is very simple and it will make her stomach feel better. But from the way she looks at me I wonder if maybe something else besides her stomach is what really hurts her.

Everybody starts to eat and drink more wine and we are running back and forth from the kitchen and around the table trying to make everybody happy. Bob wants more artichokes and Gabriella shows him how to eat them the best way. The reporter likes the chicken and wants to know if there is any more drippings. He calls it gravy. Then Stash knocks over a bottle of *chianti* on the table and everybody starts to scream and laugh and I try to mop it up. In Italy we say good luck comes to the person if they spill over some wine.

Gabriella touches some of the spilled wine from the table and she puts it behind her ears like it is perfume. Everyone thinks this is very funny, especially Bob's girls and they do it, too. Then Dean the artist gets up and she starts to dance around with her napkin like it is a veil and everyone starts to wave their napkins around. I tell you, everyone really is going crazy here. They keep eating and eating and eating and drinking and drinking and drinking and we are working like mad to keep up.

Primo goes behind Ann and he helps her with her plate. I can see she is very impressed by his cooking and she looks completely in love now. He feeds her a couple of beans off her plate and I can see that he likes her very much now and is not maybe so shy with her. Then he starts to talk with Pascal and he is even laughing with Pascal! I never think I see this for as long as I live. I think Pascal can't believe this food that Primo make. He gives Primo a lot of compliments about the dinner and I think this maybe makes Primo trust him a little more. He can see that Pascal really does understand what is good food.

Just when everybody thinks they are finished eating we go back in the kitchen. We are both very tired from running all over the place and Cristiano has already started to wash some of the dishes and he is going crazy to get them done. But we have one more dish we want to bring out. I call Cristiano to come over and together the three of us wheel out our dessert cart and on it is a whole roasted pig! This pig is unbelievable. It have an apple in the mouth and it is surrounded by fruits like grapes and pears.

When we bring this into the dining room I see some of the guests almost drop their jaws out of their heads when they see this pig. Gabriella looks at it and screams because she can't believe we have even more food. Everyone is just amazed by this and they start to clap. I hold my hands up to my brother Primo because he is the one who really cooked all of this for them.

Primo takes a bow and he starts to carve the pig up. Then Bob gets up and says he wants to try to carve the pig because he never have done this. He comes up and Primo shows him how to carve and he is pretty good with the knife. Cristiano and myself make the plates and start to serve but everyone is saying they are too full up to eat any more. I tell them they have to taste since Primo worked all day long to make this pig.

"If I eat anything else I'll just bust right open!" one of Bob's girls says to me and she puts her head down on the table.

"Well, I'll try it," Chubby says and everybody laughs because nobody is too surprised to hear him say this.

Chapter Ten

How to Play the Ring Game

Cut a piece of string so that it is several yards long. (The string should be long enough so that everyone playing the game can hold it with two hands.) Put a simple ring—such as wedding band—on the string and tie it at the ends. Everyone now gathers around in a circle and holds the string in their hands in front of them. The ring should be able to pass easily on the string from person to person. (To play this game you need at least 8 people; 10 to 15 is best.)

One person goes inside the circle and closes his or her eyes. Once the ring is hidden in someone's hand, the person in the middle can open his or her eyes and start to look for the ring. When the person in the middle thinks he or she knows where the ring is, he or she points at the person in the circle and that person must open up his or her hands to show if the ring is there. When the person in the middle finds the ring, he or she leaves the center and joins the circle, and whoever was caught with the ring goes into the middle and the play starts over again.

The goal of the people passing the ring is to keep from being caught with it. The ring can be passed in either direction and without warning. Often people in the circle will distract the person in the middle by pretending to have the ring—but they are really empty-handed. Shouting and yelling are good distractions, too.

Secondo

At our uncle's *trattoria* in Frascati, the customers like to sit and talk for a long time after they eat their meal. They drink an *espresso* or a nice glass of *grappa*, they eat a *biscotti* or they crack some nuts or have a piece of fruit. That's it, very simple. This is what we have tonight for *i dolci*, or as the Americans say, the dessert. After all the food we make you can't have too much for the dessert because you are too full. But a *caffè* and maybe a nice pastry, or sometimes a *granita* ice, is just right.

Nobody is talking too much now though because everyone is very tired. It is very late and eating this much dinner has made everyone sleepy. Everyone is all over the place. Phyllis has her head down on the table and is sleeping and Father O'Brien is nodding off in the corner in the booth. The photographer is sitting by himself at another table. I see him pick up his camera and he turns it so it faces his own face and he shoots a picture of himself with a flash. He is a strange guy, this photographer.

Mrs. Chubby is laying down right on the big table like she is the model in a painting and Stash is again sketching her in his pad. "Don't move," he says to her. "Don't worry," she says to him and laughs. "I'm too full to go anywhere."

At the end of the table I see one of Bob's girls is sitting there and crying. She is very cute this girl, she have a small face and she have her blond hair all tied up in the back in a bun. Chubby goes up behind her and he says, very quiet, "What's the matter?"

"My mother was such a terrible cook," the girl says and she cries some more.

Bob is sitting at the piano and even though he have a cast on his hand he is playing some blues music and Gabriella and Cristiano are dancing a slow dance right next to him. I think Cristiano is maybe a little bit in love with Gabriella. I don't think he ever dance with a woman like her before. In her high heels she is taller than him and he looks up at her eyes when they are dancing. Maybe Cristiano now feels a little different about *las mujeres* after tonight.

Pascal is showing some of the guests how to do the trick with the Amaretti di Saronno *biscotti*. These are cookies you get from Italy and they have papers around them and the trick works like this. You take the paper off the cookie and make it into a tube and you stand the tube up on the table. Then you light a match to the top of the tube and it burns down the paper. But just when the fire get to the bottom, the paper and the ash from the fire fly up into the sky.

"Okay, one, two, three," Pascal say and everyone lights their papers. When they fly up, everyone makes a sound and says how beautiful this look.

"Isn't that wonderful?" I hear Pascal say. It's just wonderful. Everything is just wonderful right now. No Louis Prima. Louis Prima did not come. Just like that. It makes me feel very tired. Everything we do today is for nothing. I go to the bar to get a cigarette and Jameson the reporter is sitting there finishing a glass of Sambuca. I nod hello to him.

"Look, I'll see if I can't get someone out here to do a review," he says, "but that could take a while." He drinks down the rest of his drink. "And I'm afraid I can't write a story about Louis Prima, because he didn't show up."

"I understand," I say.

Jameson looks at me and smiles. "But you were right," he says. "It was the best. Ever."

"Thank you," I say but I'm not so sure it really matters if he likes it or not now. "What time do you have?" I ask.

"God, it's three o'clock," he says. "I gotta go. Good night." He shakes my hand and he faces the table. "Good night all," he calls out to everyone.

Some of the guests call out "good night" and Jameson goes over to the booth where Primo and Ann are sitting and talking. He shakes Primo's hand and says thank you and then he goes out.

I look over at my brother. He is saying something to Ann and making her laugh very hard. Then she whispers something in his ear and he laughs. When he looks up he sees me looking at him. I go over to him.

"You enjoy yourself tonight," I say to him, very hard.

Primo shrugs his shoulders at me. I can see he is embarrassed by what I say in front of Ann but I don't care. Ann just looks down at her hands and I walk away from them. I am mad about this whole big mess.

Primo is happy right now but tomorrow when we have no money left let's see how happy he is then. I think he doesn't care about what happens because he knows I will be the one who takes care of it. I am always the one who takes care of everything and I am tired of this.

I go to the end of the table where Louis Prima and his band was supposed to sit for the dinner. The places are still set with the empty plates from the start of the meal that they never eat on. I put out the candles with my fingers by squeezing the flames and I start to pick up the dishes. Pascal sees me do this and he comes up to me. I don't want to talk to him. I don't want to talk to anybody right now.

"Listen, baby, I don't know what to say," he says. "I am so fucking embarrassed. I'm sorry."

I just nod my head at him. I barely can hear what he is saying.

"But you know what?" he goes on. "These people had a goddamn great time. You should be proud like hell."

I am proud like hell and I am mad like hell. He said Louis Prima and now no Louis Prima. I spent most of the money we have and now we have nothing. End of the story. I start to walk to the kitchen with the plates.

Pascal stops me and puts his hand on my arm. He says, "Everything will be okay, you'll see. We talk tomorrow, okay?"

"Okay," I say and walk away from him with the plates and go into the kitchen. Cristiano is leaning against the table smoking a cigarette and he looks at me when I come in. He looks tired, too. But I am so mad I say nothing to him and I take the plates that were to be for Louis Prima and his friends to the garbage pail and I throw them in, one at a time. They break and make a big crashing sound when they hit the bottom of the can. Cristiano just watches me and says nothing.

I see on the cutting board the *timpano* that was to be for Louis Prima. It is so soggy now it looks like somebody came in and sat on it. I want to throw the *timpano* in the garbage too but I leave it alone. I just want to go be by myself and not talk to anyone.

When I go back into the dining room, Primo is up on his feet and he is calling everyone to come around and play the ring game. Ann is laughing very hard at what he says. This is all that I need right now. A game.

"This is the game," he says to the room. "The ring is on the string. One person in the middle has to find the ring. Don't get caught with the ring. Very important: You must lie and cheat to not get caught with the ring!"

He makes a big circle with the string. "Come, come, get

in the circle," he says to everyone. Ann is still laughing at him and everyone starts to wake up and stand up and stretch. They all start to gather around him, laughing and talking and asking him how to play this game.

"Ann, you start," Primo says.

"Me?" Ann says.

"You get in the middle," Primo says. Everyone makes a ring around her and holds on to the string. Ann gets in the middle and she turns around and around to try and find the ring that the people are hiding with their hands and passing to each other. Everyone yells at her to confuse her about where the ring is. That's how you play the game. If you ever play this game, you know it gets very loud because people yell and pretend they have the ring. I don't want to hear this noise right now.

I go down the hall and into the bathroom. I sit on the toilet and I start to think about this night. I am stupid to think that this one night would make everything okay. I never think that Louis Prima would not show up. How come he doesn't show up? I don't know what we can do now. I have nothing left. Now we are just like any other restaurant. No stars come here, nobody come here.

I look up and Gabriella is there in the doorway. She smiles at me and comes in and leans against the wall. I nod at her and then I look down at the floor. I am embarrassed to see her right now. This afternoon at her place I play the big shot with her, like I am going to be the big success after tonight. I think now she will make fun of me.

She doesn't say nothing for a minute and then she looks down at me. I can smell her perfume. We can hear everyone laughing and having a good time playing the ring game in the other room.

"You don't like games?" she says.

"No," I say.

She nods and looks away. "They make me also tired."

I look up at her. I see lines in her face near her eyes that I never notice there before. She looks older than she is really and she looks very tired, like she has just traveled a long way on a trip.

"He was supposed to come," I say to her. She nods at me. "It would have helped. Now, to start again . . ."

I feel like I am to cry, but I stop myself. I have not cried for a long time. I don't think I have cried since my father died.

"We're left with nothing," I say to her.

Gabriella kneels down in front of me. She touches my face with her hand. "No, no, *poverino,* what are you saying?" she says. "You have so much."

She take my head in her hands and she begins to kiss my face. She feels so warm near me and I start to kiss her back. She seems different to me now, not so tough like she always is. She seems more soft and maybe a little bit sad like me.

We kiss and then I hear a noise in the doorway and we look up and there is Phyllis. *Madonna miseria.* She catches Gabriella and me kissing and she makes a little noise with her throat and then she turns and she runs away.

"Phyllis!" I call after her.

Gabriella stands up. I look at her. She says nothing but she throws her hands up to say she can't believe this happen. She's not the only one. This is all I need to happen right now. I don't say anything but I look at her to say I am going after Phyllis and she looks at me like she understands this but also she doesn't understand it at the same time.

I run out of the door of the toilet and into the dining room. I see Phyllis go out of the front door of the Paradise and I run after her. Everyone is still busy playing the ring game and doesn't notice me. As I run I hear Primo call to me but I keep on going and out the door to get Phyllis back.

Primo

I never think this dinner we make tonight will go like it go. I know what I cook will be good and I hope everyone will like it but I never think I have a good time like this. I am busy like crazy when everyone eats. I fix up *i secondi* with Seco and make sure everyone have enough of what they like. I never see a table of people enjoy what they eat so much. Is like if I have to die and go to heaven and cook there, this is how I think people will like the food I make. Everyone just eat more and more and like everything.

I also have a good time because Ann is here. Is more easy now for me to talk to her. I no am so nervous like today when I go to her shop. It seem like two year go by since this morning. After the meal we sit in a booth and talk and drink a *grappa* and a *caffè*. She tell me a funny story about her shop and the customer who come in and complain about this flower or that flower or why can she no have tulip for them in the winter. You can't get a tulip in the winter! She say sometimes her customer no understand and I say I know what she mean, this happen to me too all the time. She work hard, Ann, just like me.

Now everyone at the party is tired because they eat so much. Some people are fall asleep so I think to wake up everybody with the ring game. This is a game we play in my family in Italia and I think it to be very funny. You put a ring on a big piece of the string and make a big circle and put somebody in the middle who must find the ring. Everyone have to lie and cheat and pretend to have the ring even if they don't. Because that is how you keep from going inside the middle.

I tell Ann to go in the middle first because she never play this game before and I think she will like. She is very good because only a minute go by and she find the ring. I am the one who have the ring but I force Pascal next to me to take it at the last second and Ann catch him. So Pascal is caught and he have to go in the middle next.

Everyone is laugh and have a good time. After Pascal find the ring with one of Bob's girls I see Phyllis go from the circle and to the bathroom. This girl of Bob's is not too smart and she take a long time to find the ring and she is very funny because she make this noise like a mouse when she can't find it. Everyone laugh so hard when she make this noise. She look like a mouse too, she is small, this girl.

I look up from the game and I see Phyllis come run from the bathroom and then Secondo come run after her. I think something to be wrong.

"Che c'è?" I call to him, but he just keep on running and he go out the front door after her. I think they maybe have some fight or something. What else can be new? But then I see Gabriella come out of the bathroom too and I wonder what is go on. Something no so good because she no look very happy.

Gabriella come to the bar where we play the game and she stand near me and Pascal. She take her lipstick from her purse and she fix her lips and she look at Pascal.

"What's the matter?" Pascal call to her from the circle.

"I gotta go," she say.

"Why?"

"I'm going," she say.

Bob hear her and call out to her, "No, c'mon, Gabriella, stay," and someone else call out, "Yeah, we're waiting for Louis Prima," and everyone laughs at this. We all know Louis Prima is not coming this late.

"Yeah, Louis Prima, don't hold your breath," she say quiet but mean and I think only me and Pascal hear her say this. Pascal let go of the string and look at her like he is surprise when she say this. She look back at him like she is mad with him. Her dark eyes flash at him.

"What? What do you want with me?" she say to him and then she point her finger at me. "Tell your new friend here about who's coming tonight."

I am confuse by this. "What do you say?" I ask her.

"Tell him," she say to Pascal. "He's worked very hard."

Pascal look down at feet and he say, "Okay, okay."

"What?" I say. I let go the string, too. Everybody is still playing the game, very fast and very loud. Nobody is pay any attention to what we say.

"We should go," Pascal say to Gabriella and he walk over to her. "Let's go now."

"Tell your new friend," she say to him again and she point at me. She is angry now.

"No, we're going," Pascal say and he start to walk to the door. "C'mon."

Gabriella come up close to me and look at me in my eyes. She give a little smile to me that look sad.

"No one's coming tonight," she says, "no one ever was coming." She kiss me on the cheek and she take my arm with her hand. "Thank you for the best meal I will probably ever have," she say.

She go over to Pascal and she stand there and she look at him for a minute. She no say nothing to him. He just stare back at her. Then she walk past him and go out the door.

I can't believe what she say to me. I look over at Pascal so he can tell me what she mean. Pascal just stand there and he stare at me. He give to me a shrug and a little smile like he is a little boy who get caught taking some candy when he is not supposed to. Then he turn around and he walk out the door.

All I can think is about Secondo. I try to tell him that this Pascal is no good. I always know this about Pascal because I see the food he serve to his customer. He lie to them with his food. You can't lie with the food you make because then this

is like you lie to yourself. But Seco give Pascal his trust anyway. And now Pascal lie to him.

I think I must go outside and find my brother. Stash
come over to me and ask me what is go on. I tell him I am
go to find Seco and I go out the door to look for him.

Secondo

Once I get outside the Paradise I see Phyllis running
down the street toward the ocean and she is very fast, I can't
believe how fast she is. I am tired from working on the party
all day and I can't run very fast. She goes over the dune and
down the beach and when I get to the top of the dune I look
down and I see she has taken off her shoes and pulled her
dress off and she is going into the water.

I call after her but she just keeps on going. What is she
going into the water for in the middle of the night? *Madonna
miseria.* Then she is swimming out in the waves. There is a
big moon shining down on the water but no light comes from
anywhere else except from the little lamps on the pier. I can
just see her head bobbing up and down in the waves. She
looks so small out there in the dark water, like a drop of milk
in a cup of coffee.

"Phyllis! Phyllis!" I yell out to her. "What are you
doing?"

I go down to the edge of the ocean. I don't want to get
too close to the water because I don't want my shoes to get
wet. She keeps swimming in the water and she doesn't answer me.

"Phyllis! Come here!" I call to her. "I want to talk to
you!"

I see her go under the water. Oh my God. What is she

doing? She stays underneath the water a minute and then I see her splash up again.

"Phyllis, please! What are you doing?" I yell. "You're going to catch cold!" Now I am start to get nervous about her being out there. This water must be cold like ice.

Finally she starts to swim toward the shore and then she stands up out of the water. She walks toward me very slow. She is wearing only her white slip now and she looks like a beautiful Greek statue that becomes alive or maybe like the Venus in the Botticelli painting who comes out of the water. She seems very tall to me all of a sudden.

"Phyllis, what are you doing?" I say when she gets close to me.

She gives me a very strange kind of smile, like she is almost laughing at me. She reaches down into the water and she splashes it at me.

"Don't get wet!" she says and she laughs at me and she starts to run away. I chase after her and she is very fast again and she runs around in circles. Every time I get close to her she changes her direction and goes running to another part of the beach. I try to keep up and when I catch up to her I am all out of breath. I am behind her and I take her by the arm.

"Phyllis," I say, "I was just upset, and she—"

"No!" she yells at me, very loud. She pushes herself away from my arm. "Don't do that!" she says. "I hate that!"

"Okay, okay," I say. I didn't think she would take this for an excuse but I think that if I start here she will not be so upset. I want to explain about Gabriella even though I know there is nothing to explain to her that she wants to hear.

"Can I just talk to you for one minute?" I say. She just stares at me, but now she doesn't look angry at me anymore. Her face looks very calm and peaceful like she just woke up from a long sleep. Her hair and her slip are dripping with water.

"No, you can't," she says in a very quiet voice and she pushes some hair out of her face. "You're too late. I'm not here anymore."

Then she turns away and she walks away from me. I can't go after her now. What can I say to her? She saw me kissing Gabriella and that's it. Anything I can say about this would be not enough or too much. There is nothing to explain. I just have to let her go now.

I look up the dune and I see Primo standing there. Then I see Cristiano coming over the top of the dune. Phyllis goes to where she left her dress and her shoes in a pile in the sand and she picks them up and she starts to walk up the dune. She stops when she gets to Primo and he touches her on her cheek. But she doesn't say anything to him and she keeps walking up the dune.

When she gets to Cristiano I see him take off his new waiter's jacket and he puts it around her shoulders. All of a sudden she puts her arms around him and gives him a hug. Cristiano doesn't know what is going on and he looks amazed by this. Then she lets go and keeps walking and she goes to the top of the dune. I see Alberto and Ida are there now and so is Ann. Phyllis just walks by them without saying a word to them.

I can't look at any of them anymore. I turn away and I stare out at the black water. I know I am a fool. First, no Louis Prima. Now no Phyllis. I am a fool.

Primo

When I go out of the Paradise I don't know where Secondo and Phyllis go but I remember I see Phyllis run by the front window when she leave the restaurant so I go down the street to where the beach begin. I go to the top of the sand and I look out and see something down on the beach. I go down a little bit and there is Seco run after Phyllis all around on the beach. The wind is blow pretty hard so I can't hear what she say when she yell at him. I see he say something to her and she say something back and then she walk away from him.

She come up the beach to me and I want to ask her what is the matter but when she stop she just look at me very sad and say nothing. I touch her on her face. She is crying. Then she just go by me and keep walking. I look down at Seco. He stand there on the beach and he look like he is a little boy. I go down to him.

When I reach him he is face out to the water. I know he and Phyllis have a big fight and I can tell from the way she walk away from him this is probably the last fight they have for good. I stand behind him and look out at the water, too. The wind is blow less here at the edge of the water. I look across the ocean but you can see nothing except water and more water and the big moon hang over. It look like a big onion when you cut it in half and it make you cry.

"He is not coming," I say to Seco. He no say nothing. I can't see his face so I don't know if he understand what I say or no.

"Seco," I say.

"What?"

"Pascal never call," I say. He no say nothing again and he stand very still. Then he say, "What do you mean?"

"Pascal never call him," I say. "So he is not coming."

"How do you know this?"

"Gabriella," I say. I look out at the water again and I can see Seco puts his head down. "Pascal lied to you. He lied."

Seco is quiet for a time and then he turn around. But he no look at me. He say, "Where is everybody? I should go say something."

He start to go and he wave to me and say, "C'mon."

"No," I say, "no more." But Seco keep on walk away from me. I think now is the time to tell him what I talk to our uncle about. We must do something if we have no more money left for the Paradise. All this stupid business with Pascal and Louis Prima. This is not why we come here to this country. We come here to have a good restaurant, we no come here to play games. Pascal and his kind just want to play games, they want to lie and pretend. I no want to pretend. I no think Seco really want to pretend either. I want to say to him that we must go back now.

"Secondo," I say, and he stop walking and look at me. This is hard for me to say to him because I know he want to stay here, he want to make money, he want to be a success. But I have to tell him this.

"There is a job," I say. "*Senti,* just listen."

He looks at me to go on.

"With Uncle Paolo," I say. "His new place, in Roma. I talk to him. I called him. He say both of us. If you want."

I am nervous to tell him this and I laugh. Seco look at me and he no say nothing for a second and I think he is to be mad. But then he smile at me. "Good," he say.

I can't believe this is what he say. "Good?" I ask and he start to nod at me and he say, "Sure, good." I touch his arm and I say, "Good."

He point his finger at me. "You go back," he say to me. "I am going to stay here."

"No, no, Secondo," I say. Uncle Paolo say both of us and I want us to go back home both of us together.

"You want to go back?" he say. "Okay, good, you go back. Fuck him. And fuck you. You go back there. You let somebody else take care of you."

He walk away from me. "No, Secondo!" I call after him. I am mad now. What is he say? I am the one who take care of him! He run around here in America, Mr. Big Shot, Mr. Cadillac, and look where it get us to be.

"Good, go on, stay!" I yell to him. "You go on! Stay! Go! Stay!"

He is keep walking up the beach. I am boiling like a pot on the stove. I yell out to him, "You have rotted, Secondo!"

When he hear this he stop and he turn around to me fast. "What? What did you say?" he say and he come run to me.

"You have rotted!" I yell again.

When he get to me he stop and he screw up his face and it get very red.

"No! You!" he scream at me and point his finger again. "You are the one! You are the one! You think things are so simple, huh?! You think it is just like this and like that?! And there is nothing in the middle?! Is that what you think!?"

"No, no!" I yell at him.

"Who the fuck do you think you are?!" Now he is yelling so hard I think he is about to cry. His voice go up and up. "You do nothing! You have your head in the pot and you do nothing! I did something! We were dying and I did something! For two years, I have been doing it all! I ask you for help! I need you to sacrifice! And you give to me nothing!"

He is a crazy man now. He know no what he say to me. "That's what you think?" I yell.

"Yes!" he say.

"That I give to you nothing!"

"Yes! You give to me nothing!" he yell and he kick some sand at me. "Nothing!"

He give me a wave with his hand and he start to walk away from me. I am so angry now I don't know what to do. Before I know what I do I run over to him very fast and try to grab him and throw him down on the ground. But he grab me back and we push each other away. Then he try to kick me. I try to kick him back and he start to kick sand at me and I run at him and grab him and we fall down to the ground. We start to roll around in the sand and first I am on top of him and then he is on top of me and I try to punch him but he keep move away from me and then he just stand up. I have sand in my face and in my hair and mouth and I stand up on my knees. I grab the sand with my hands and throw it at the sky.

"Questo posto!" I yell at him. *"Questo posto ci mangia vivi!"* This place is eat us alive!

"Good, good!" he scream at me and he start to walk away from me again but I get up and go after him and I grab him again.

"Where are you go?!" I yell at him. "Where do you want to go? You always want to leave!"

We are both tire now but I grab his shirt and I throw him down to the ground. He try to get up but I push him down again and I put my foot on his chest so he can't move.

"Stay! Stay still for one minute!" I say to him but I am breathing very fast and is hard for me to talk. "I try to teach you, Secondo, but you never learn! You act like a child! You make me take care of you! Why do you act like this? Why? Why do you want to stay here?"

I go to my knees. I am too upset now to try to explain everything to him and I start to punch the sand again. I punch it very hard. "This place is eating us alive!" I scream at him again and then I punch the sand again with my hand and this time I punch too hard and I hurt my hand. I scream in pain from the hit and I fall on the ground. Seco try to grab on to me but I push him away and I crawl away from him. I am holding my hand because it hurt like somebody hit it with a hammer.

I am now all out of breath and Seco is breathe hard too. I lie on the ground and I look up at the night. I think how big the night look. The moon is very light and I can see the stars shine in the black sky. Seco crawl over to me and he try to take my hand but I pull it away from him.

"Primo, *basta*," he say. "*Basta*. Let me see your hand." I let him take my hand but I close my eyes to my brother. I can't look at him now.

"You want me to make a sacrifice," I say to him. "No. When I sacrifice my work, it dies. Is better that I die."

I get up from the sand. He is still on the ground. I start to walk away and I see Ann is stand there and is look at us. "Primo, Primo," I hear my brother call to me from the ground but I keep walking. The wind is blow hard now and Seco's voice sound far away from me, like in the dream I have today in the barber chair when my brother chase me. Only this time is no dream. I go to Ann and she take my arm. We walk away from Seco and she take me down the beach.

Chapter Eleven

Secondo's Eggs

Uova di Secondo

Take 4 big eggs and break them into a bowl. Whisk them together until they are well blended and add a big pinch of salt. Put a good frying pan on the stove and turn the heat up to medium high. Add a dash of extra virgin olive oil, just enough to coat the bottom of the pan.

When the oil is warm pour in the eggs and stir with a wooden spoon to mix. Let the eggs cook until the bottom is set. Then stir a little bit or tilt the pan so that the uncooked parts go to the bottom of the pan and cook, but do not scramble the eggs. When the eggs are firm, take the pan off the fire. Serves three people.

Secondo

I am alone on the beach. I am sweating and I have sand in my shoes, in my hair, everywhere. My shoulder hurts from fighting with Primo. I sit up in the sand and I take off my jacket. I look it over to see if there are any rips. It has stains from the sand but nothing is torn up.

I will go to get Pascal. Everything bad has happened because of him. I don't know what I will do when I get him, but I think I will probably try to kill him. How could I trust Pascal? Why would he help me? I am a fool to trust him, I am *stupido*. Now he has made everything fall apart. He lied to me.

I walk up the beach and over the dune and up the street to the Paradise. It is very late now and everything is quiet. I see Bob in his Cadillac. One of his girls is sitting next to him and they are laughing about something. The other girl is in the backseat and she is passed out.

"Hey, Secondo," Bob calls to me as I walk by his black Cadillac. "It was a great party even if . . . well, can I take you somewhere?"

"No, thanks, Bob," I say.

"Okay, see ya," Bob says. He starts his car up and he puts it in gear and he drives away. He waves to me as he goes down the hill toward the water. I stand for a second and I watch his car go around the bend. The red taillights get smaller and smaller and then I can't see them anymore.

I start to walk over to Pascal's but when I pass in front of the Paradise I hear piano music coming from inside the restaurant. I wonder if any other guests are still here so I think I should go say good night to them before I go see Pascal. I even think that maybe it is Louis Prima come after all, but that is just for one second because Louis Prima is a lie.

The music is a kind of waltz, very strange, slow and pretty. When I go in the door I see the restaurant is mostly dark and everyone is gone home. I walk past the bar and I turn the corner to where the piano is and there is Pascal. He is the one playing the piano.

I stand there and stare at him, but he just keeps on playing. He plays this song very good. I never know he can play the piano. Pascal looks up at me and he stops.

"I used to play at one time," he says to me.

"You ruin me," I say.

Pascal nods and he goes back to play on some of the keys for a second.

"Because of a woman?" I ask. I think that it must be because of Gabriella. He found out about what we do and this is how he get back at me, he makes me lose my shirt.

But Pascal makes a little laugh and says, "Seco, please, be serious."

"Then why?" I feel like I am standing on the edge of a high cliff and if I take one step I will go flying down. I stay very still.

Pascal shrugs at me. "Because I wanted to save you," he says.

"And then we would go with you?" I say.

"Where else would you go?" he says and shrugs again. He hits some keys again. So he have a plan. All of this was a plan from the start, when I go to see him in his office. He knew I would do anything to stop from drowning. So he make sure we are all the way under the water and then he can come and pull us out and be the big hero.

Pascal stops playing and looks up at me.

"What I did, I did out of respect," he says. "He is a great investment, your brother. And you, too, of course."

I go for him and he stands up fast from the piano, kicking the bench out behind him. I stand right in front of him. I want to spit in his face. I lean my face in close to his.

"You would never have my brother," I say. "He lives in a world above you. What he has and what he is, is rare. You are nothing."

Pascal stares right back at me and he doesn't blink.

"I am a businessman, baby," he says, very quiet. "I am anything I need to be at any time. Tell me, what exactly are you?"

He walks past me and out to the door. I think I should go after him but what he says to me stops me. I know it will do nothing to go and fight with him. He will still be Pascal and he will do what he did to me and my brother the same way to the next guys who come along. People like him go on and on and you can't stop them no matter what you try to do. I hear the door slam and then I am alone in the restaurant.

I look around at everything. The place look like somebody have a war here. There are chairs all over the place and dirty dishes on the table and coffee cups and crumbs and spilled wine and the flowers are wilted already. I work goddamn hard for this place for two years and now it is nothing. Just a big mess that have to be cleaned up.

I pull out a chair from the head of the dinner table and I sit down. I am so tired. I don't want to think about anything anymore. I close my eyes and I put my head down on my arms. I go to sleep.

Big Night

Primo

I feel the sand pinch my feet in my shoe like a crab when we walk away from Seco. Ann ask me if I am okay and if I am hurt and I say no. I still have a pain in my hand from where I hit the sand but I say nothing about this. She no ask me any more question. She no say nothing else to me. She take my arm and she pull me close to her and she lead me. I no even know where I am go to.

Ann have a little house just up from the beach. In the front yard she have a garden but is too dark for me to see much of it. When we go inside her house it smell like her. She tell me to sit down in a big chair and take off my shoe. I just do what she say. I take off my shoe and I am think about Seco. I no understand why he want to stay here when this place is no good for us. We can't go on like this. *Non possiamo andare avanti cosi.*

Ann bring me a cup of tea and she say, "Here, drink this." It smell like mint leaf. I sip some of this tea and it make me feel better.

"Are you sure you're all right?" she say. I look up at her and I nod. I stand up and take her hand. I put my arm around her waist and I smile at her and I kiss her. She put her arm around me and she hug me very tight. I put my face in her neck and kiss it very soft and I feel how warm she is. I want to make love to her and I feel she want to too. She take my hand and she lead me down the hallway to her bedroom.

"I'll be just a minute," she say and she go into the bathroom. I sit on the bed. Is dark in her room because she no put any lights on. Is a long time since I am with a woman and I am a little bit nervous.

Since we come here to this country, my brother has all the time try to get me to go out and see girls and meet them, but I want to stay in my kitchen. Now I am here with Ann I remember what it is like to be with someone and it is nice. I know Seco just want me to be happy here but this is hard for me when people no understand the food I make and when people lie and cheat like Pascal. But Seco bring me and Ann together. I know he think if I am with someone here I no will want to go back to Italy. I don't know about this. If we have no money I no see how we can stay here. I don't know what will happen to us now.

Ann open the door to the bathroom and the light come into the bedroom. She stand in the doorway and she have a nightgown on. She look like an angel. She turn out the light and she come over to me. I put my arm around her and hold her and press my face against her breast. She start to fall on top of me and then we are on the bed together and we start to kiss each other all over.

Secondo

When I wake up I am still at the big table. I look at my watch. It is seven in the morning. I don't know how but the first thing I think about is food. I am hungry. I think I ate nothing last night I was so busy with the meal and the guests and everything else.

I go in the kitchen and there I see Cristiano is asleep. He is stretched out on the table in the back of the stove. He must have fallen asleep after he was cleaning everything up. I am very proud of him. He did a very good job as a waiter. He is still a little slow, but he is young and he need to practice more. Too bad, I don't think he will get too much practice at the Paradise anymore.

I don't know where my brother is. I don't think he has come home yet. In all our life, I don't know he has even been out all night until the morning. But now it is morning. The sun is coming up and I can hear the birds singing outside in the backyard.

When I walk past Cristiano he opens up his eyes and he wakes up.

"Good morning," I say to him. He sits up on the table and rubs his eyes like a little child.

"Morning," he says.

I get a bowl of eggs from underneath the side table.

"Are you hungry?" I ask him.

He nods and then he jumps off the butcher block table like he wants to do something to help me.

"I do it," I tell him. I take down a frying pan from the rack and put it on the stove and turn the heat on high underneath. I put some olive oil in the pan. In America everyone uses butter to cook eggs but my stomach don't like butter very much. Then I take four eggs and break them into a bowl. I stir them up with a fork very fast and add some salt. I pour the eggs into the pan and it make a big sizzle noise. I mix up the eggs a little bit in the pan and turn the heat down some so they don't burn.

Cristiano gets some bread in a basket from last night and he sits on the butcher block with his long legs hanging off it. He eats some bread. I go to the shelf and get a plate for him and a plate for me and some forks and I put them on the table by the stove.

When I go back to the stove the eggs are almost done. I pat them with a wooden spoon to make sure they are cooked all the way through. Then I turn off the heat and pick up the pan and bring it to the table. I give some eggs to me and some to Cristiano and put the rest back on the stove. I give Cristiano his plate and some more bread and he say thanks and he starts to eat. I sit at the table and start to eat my eggs, too. We don't say anything.

I don't want to think about anything right now. I just want to eat the eggs. They taste very good to me, like it is the first time I ever eat eggs in my life. I don't know what I am going to do now about anything.

Then I hear the back door open and I look up and there is Primo come into the kitchen. He doesn't say nothing. He just stands there looking at us. He looks like he is not slept at all and his hair is all messed up and the jacket of his chef whites is opened up. He looks like the stray dog who smells the food from outside the kitchen and wanders in hoping he can get some meat from the chef.

I get up and go to the shelf again and I get another plate. I go to the stove and I put the rest of the eggs in the pan on the plate and put it down next to my plate on the table. I put the basket with the bread next to the plate and then I sit back down and go back to eating my eggs.

Primo stands there for another second like he doesn't know what to do. Then he takes a chair from the corner and puts it next to mine. He sits down and he starts to eat his eggs and from the way he eats them I can tell he is very hungry, too.

I don't know what I can say to him. I think we say what we have to say last night on the beach. We sit and eat our eggs and he doesn't say anything to me, so I don't say anything, too.

But I want to say I am sorry so I put my hand on his shoulder and then I put it around to his other shoulder. I can tell he wants to say he is sorry too and he puts his arm around my shoulder, too. I think Cristiano sees this because he gets off the butcher block and he takes his plate of eggs and he goes out the door to the outside. The light from the morning comes in when he opens the door.

My brother and me take our arms down and we eat our eggs some more. For right now we do not look at each other. We just go on eating together.

Made in the USA
Lexington, KY
27 November 2012